"Why did you kiss me?"

For a moment he looked startled.
"Why does any man kiss a woman?"

"You're a man, so you tell me."

His gaze lingering on her mouth, he said quizzically, "Usually because he can't resist the temptation."

"Well, I've no intention of having an affair with you."

"What makes you think I want an affair?"

Feeling incredibly foolish, she stammered, "I—I'm sorry, but I thought..."

"I want to marry you."

LEE WILKINSON lives with her husband in a three-hundred-year-old stone cottage in a Derbyshire village, which most winters gets cut off by snow. They both enjoy traveling and recently, joining forces with their daughter and son-in-law, spent a year going around the world "on a shoestring" while their son looked after Kelly, their much-loved German shepherd dog. Her hobbies are reading and gardening and holding impromptu barbecues for her long-suffering family and friends.

Also on sale this month *A Vengeful Deception* by Lee Wilkinson, Harlequin Presents #2264

Books by Lee Wilkinson

HARLEQUIN PRESENTS®
2228—MARRIAGE ON THE AGENDA

Ruthless!

LEE WILKINSON

THE MILLIONAIRES

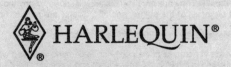

TORONTO • NEW YORK • LONDON
AMSTERDAM • PARIS • SYDNEY • HAMBURG
STOCKHOLM • ATHENS • TOKYO • MILAN • MADRID
PRAGUE • WARSAW • BUDAPEST • AUCKLAND

ISBN 0-373-80519-5

RUTHLESS!

First North American Publication 2002.

Copyright © 1996 by Lee Wilkinson.

Visit us at www.eHarlequin.com

Printed in U.S.A.

CHAPTER ONE

HER excitement mingling with a strange apprehension that amounted almost to a premonition, Lisa glanced around the bustling international arrivals lounge at New York's John F. Kennedy airport.

With only a few boyhood snapshots to go by, recognising Mark wasn't going to prove easy. Of course *he* would be looking out for *her*, but with even less to go on it would be harder for him.

Perhaps they should have arranged to wear red noses or hold a balloon aloft, she thought, her usual sunny self surfacing briefly.

Through a gap in the moving throng she caught a glimpse of a man with black hair and a lean, strong-boned face. Dressed in a lightweight business suit, he had the physique of an athlete—broad-shouldered and narrow-hipped. He seemed to be scanning the crowd, looking for someone.

She had no real memory of Mark, and it was difficult to tell from photographs, but surely he was fairer than that?

As she stared at the man his dark eyes singled her out and she felt a quick pull of attraction, as though she had been drawn willy-nilly into his magnetic field.

A sudden bump as another luggage trolley swung against hers claimed her attention.

"Sorry." The apology was instant, the accent as English as her own. "Can't seem to keep control of the dratted thing." The fair, pleasant-faced young man tussling with his loaded trolley added, "It has a most disconcerting tendency to lean sideways."

Lisa chuckled. "I know just what you mean. Mine has a list to starboard too."

He grinned boyishly. "Still, it's one way to meet people." His eyes wandered appreciatively over her slim figure, clad in an oatmeal-coloured button-through dress with a flame-coloured scarf knotted loosely around her throat. "Would you care to share a taxi? Or are you waiting for someone?"

"Waiting for someone."

"Lucky someone." Finally succeeding in wresting his trolley free, he smiled at her before moving on.

Most people smiled at Lisa, even the grumpy ones; it was as though the sparkling hazel eyes, the happy-natured look lifted their spirits.

"Lisa Hayward?" The voice was low-pitched and fascinating with its faint Southern drawl.

She turned to find the broad-shouldered man who had caught her eye a few moments before by her side. He was much taller than she was—six feet at least, she judged, to her five feet three inches—and, close to, even more overpoweringly attractive.

His thick black hair was brushed smooth, but without the severe discipline would undoubtedly have curled. His thickly lashed eyes were beautiful—a clear dark green with even darker rims to the irises.

Gazing up into those eyes made her abruptly breathless. "Mark?" she queried, with butterflies beginning to dance in her stomach. He was in his early thirties, she guessed—about the right age, but somehow she didn't *want* this man to be her brother.

He looked down at her, studying the heart-shaped face with its dimpled chin and flawless complexion, the small, neat nose and wide mouth, the bright eyes and the riot of

silky brown curls, before answering, "I'm afraid not. But
I am here to meet you."

"Oh…" Relief and a sudden, inexplicable joy brought
a radiant smile.

She was wondering how he'd managed to pick her out
so unerringly—were she and Mark alike?—when he held
out a strong, tanned hand. "I'm Thornton Landers."

The name was vaguely familiar, but she couldn't pin
down why. There was an infinitesimal pause while he
watched her face, as though he half expected her to rec-
ognise it, before he went on, "My friends call me Thorn,"
and gave her a smile of such devastating charm that she
blinked.

Her hand clasped in his, her senses zinging from his
touch and that stunning smile, she stared into his dark,
handsome face until, realising that she was gawking at him
like some overgrown schoolgirl, she withdrew her hand and
asked quickly, "What do your enemies call you?"

"Ruthless."

The word was spoken lightly, but an odd little shiver ran
down her spine. Yes, she could well believe it, she thought.
Beneath the breathtaking charm she could sense a relent-
lessness, a steely implacability that made him formidable.

Lisa shivered again, for no good reason.

As though sensing her reaction he said smoothly, "But
I'm quite sure we'll be friends." Taking control of the recalcitrant trolley, he raised a level black brow. "Shall we
get moving?"

Outside, the dusty air was laden with diesel fumes and
the smell of hot metal and tarmac, but the June evening
was still warm and sunny, the sky an innocent baby blue.

It would be the middle of the night back home in
England, Lisa reminded herself with a sense of surprise.

She was sitting beside him in his sleek silver Mercedes,

the organised chaos of the airport left behind them, before
he asked, "What kind of a flight did you have?"

"The man next to me described it as boring, but I
thought it was fun. Though I don't watch television unless
I have to, I loved all those tiny screens on the seat-backs,
and the plastic trays of food they bring you."

His mouth twitched in amusement.

She flushed a little. He must think her very naïve and
foolish. "It was the first time I'd flown." She was annoyed
with herself for sounding defensive. "Or, at least, the first
time I can *remember*."

"I understand you were born in the States?"

"Yes—yes, I was… But when my mother—" she managed to keep her voice steady "—took me to England I
was only three."

And since then she'd lived a very quiet and ordinary life,
her books and her dreams her only means of escape.

It might well have gone on being quiet and ordinary if,
out of the blue, Mark hadn't got in touch. The letter had
been addressed to her mother, telling of her father's fatal
heart attack.

Lisa had written back with her own sad news of their
mother's death and a few days later another letter had arrived, expressing his regret.

I shall always be sorry for not keeping in touch with
you both these past years. Now it's too late…

I don't suppose you can remember me at all. I remember you as a small, curly-haired child. You used
to toddle alongside me holding onto one finger, and
when I sat down you'd climb on my knee, put your
thumb in your mouth, and go to sleep…

But, of course, that was a long time ago… Tell me
what you're doing at the moment. Are you on your
own now Mother's dead?

On discovering Lisa's circumstances, he'd written again, suggesting that she come over to New York...

As things stand the least I can do is find you a job and somewhere to live. If you don't like it over here you can always go back to England, and you'll be no worse off...

With no other family left, and grief still shrouding her bright spirit, she'd jumped at the chance of joining the brother she scarcely remembered.

As they headed due west towards Manhattan, through Queens' pleasant, mostly residential areas, they were driving into the setting sun. The low golden light made a hazy, bright tunnel, and gilded trees and buildings alike with a Midas touch.

But Lisa hardly noticed her surroundings. She was following her train of thought, until a question recurred that made her surface to ask curiously, "Are Mark and I alike?"

The top half of his face shaded by the sun visor, her companion gave her a quick glance. "No, not at all."

"Then how did you manage to pick me out so easily? I mean, there was an awful crowd and quite a few women travelling alone."

For a split second he looked disconcerted, as though the sudden question had thrown him. Then he said casually, "You were obviously looking for someone, so I took a chance."

A slight frown tugged her winged brows together. There was something curiously unsatisfactory about his answer.

Dismissing the absurd suspicion that he wasn't telling the truth—why on earth should he lie to her?—she said lightly, "I take it you're a friend of Mark's?"

"More a business colleague," he answered coolly.

"Then you're working for him?"

"At the moment he's working for me." The statement was flat and uncompromising, his curt words at variance with that soft drawl.

"Oh..." She had understood that now their father was dead Mark owned CMH Electronics.

As though regretting his brusqueness the man beside her explained, "Landers Holdings have bought him out."

Belatedly she recognised the name Landers as belonging to a large international company. And *he* was Thornton Landers, the big boss—a whizkid who by the time he was thirty had made himself a multimillionaire in his own right, quite apart from inheriting his father's business interests.

Gossip columnists mourned that not much was known about him. He strenuously guarded his privacy and was something of an enigma in a world where self-promotion was part of the business. The one thing the Press were sure of, and reiterated frequently, was that he was a tough and hard-headed businessman.

Lisa felt a small, unpleasant shock. No wonder he'd expected her to know his name.

Speculating on just how badly she'd put her foot in it, a shade stiffly she apologised. "I'm sorry. I wasn't aware you'd taken over."

"Don't worry," he told her sardonically. "You're not alone in not knowing. The news hasn't broken yet."

The words held a kind of bitter triumph that puzzled her. Even more puzzling, however, was how a man like Thornton Landers came to be meeting her.

About to blurt out the question, Lisa thought better of it and remarked obliquely, "It's very good of you to meet me, Mr Landers."

"My pleasure." He turned his head, and briefly his green eyes smiled straight into hers. "And, as we're going to be friends, please call me Thorn."

Lisa was swamped by a tidal wave of attraction, and it

was a moment or two before she was able to shake herself mentally and try again. "I thought...Mark thought...he'd be able to come himself..." The unspoken query hung on the air.

Thorn answered it. "A last-minute change of plan prevented it. Some urgent business cropped up and he had to leave for Hong Kong this morning."

"Leave for Hong Kong?" she echoed. "You mean he's not in New York?"

Pulling herself together, she shook her head. "No, don't answer that. If he had to leave for Hong Kong this morning then of course he's not in New York. You must think I'm an idiot, but I wasn't expecting him to be away and I'm..." Suddenly on my own and feeling a little let down, a little apprehensive...

"A bit tired and flustered?" he suggested, when she stayed silent. "And no doubt disappointed that I'm here instead of your brother?"

No, she wasn't disappointed. Confused, rocked by *who* he was, yes—but that instant attraction had been so strong, so powerful, that even though she knew it could come to nothing "disappointed' was the last word she would have used.

Finding her voice, she asked the question that had bothered her earlier. "Why *are* you here?"

He slanted her a glance. "I thought we'd established that I came to meet you." All at once he was making fun of her, his green eyes dancing beguilingly.

Her heart did a backward somersault and began to flap about like a stranded fish. "I mean why are *you* here?" In an attempt to hide the disturbing effect he had on her, she observed with studied mockery, "It can't be usual for the great Thornton Landers to run errands for his staff."

There was a small, frozen silence.

Perhaps, like many macho men, he had no sense of hu-

mour? Or had he thought that she was being intentionally
rude?

She was about to apologise when, surprising her, he
laughed—a nice, infectious laugh. ''I must remember to put
you over my knee for that when I get to know you better.''

A queer constriction in her throat, Lisa managed flip-
pantly, ''As it's not on the cards I won't lose any sleep
over it.''

''What's not on the cards?''

''That you'll get to know me better.''

She saw his black brows rise a fraction. ''Why do you
say that?''

''Well, once you've dropped me at Mark's apartment—''

''His apartment is empty, and he'll be away for at least
three weeks, so I won't be dropping you there.''

''Oh...'' Thinking uneasily of how few American dollars
were in her purse, she asked, ''Then you're taking me to a
hotel?''

As they drew up behind a stream of traffic waiting at a
red light, he answered blandly, ''No. I've arranged for you
to stay at my place—''

She was trying to swallow the choking excitement when
he glanced at her and added, ''So I can keep an eye on
you.''

He could have been speaking to a child.

Stung, forgetting her earlier feeling of dismay at being
alone, she informed him indignantly, ''I don't need an eye
kept on me. I'm a grown woman.''

Thorn's gaze dropped to the soft curve of her breast,
lovingly outlined by the silky material of her shirtwaister,
and lingered there for a moment.

She shivered. It was as erotic as if he'd reached over and
undone the buttons.

A glint in his eye, he remarked softly, ''I won't deny

you're a grown woman…'' Watching the hot colour pour into her cheeks, he continued with a bite, ''But as far as a city like New York is concerned you're a babe-in-arms, and I feel responsible for making sure you're safe and protected.''

In a tone intended to be withering, she fought back. ''It's very noble of you, but I can't for the life of me understand why *you* feel responsible.''

The lights changed to green, and they had travelled half a block before he admitted, ''It was because of me that your brother had to go abroad and couldn't be here to take care of you himself.''

He sounded well satisfied rather than regretful, she thought wryly. But then, if the Press were to be believed, he let nothing stand in the way of business…

All at once it struck her that though she knew a little about his public image she knew absolutely nothing of his private life. With an odd sinking feeling she realised that he might well have a wife and children.

''Are you married?'' The bald question was out before she could think better of it.

''Is that a proposal?''

''Of course not! I just—'' Recognising belatedly that he was teasing her, she stopped short, biting her lip.

''Wanted some reassurance?'' he suggested.

Lisa saw his white teeth flash in a smile, and knew that he meant reassurance that he *wasn't*.

Had she been unable to hide the effect he had on her? Or did he believe that every female was hoping to hook him? Both, probably, she thought wryly.

Carefully she answered, ''Well, a spot of reassurance wouldn't go amiss. After all, I really know nothing about you…'' At his quick sideways glance she got her pin ready to prick his over-inflated ego. ''So you can't blame me for hoping that you're safely married.''

He made the gesture of a fencer acknowledging a successful riposte. "But I'm afraid I have to destroy your hopes. I have no wife, no children." Wickedly he added, "And no current mistress. At the moment I'm quite alone."

"Oh." She felt absurdly pleased, as though she'd just received a present.

"So you'll have to take me on trust. Does that worry you?"

"Should it?"

"Perhaps it should. As you yourself pointed out, you know nothing about me. You only have my word that everything's above board and I am who I say I am. I could be a baddy in the act of abducting you."

Though he spoke lightly, there was something in his tone—a disturbing nuance—that caused the short hairs on the back of her neck to rise.

But of course he was doing it purposely, hoping to fluster her, to gain an advantage.

Calmly she answered, "You *could*. But I've no money, no connections, so I fail to see what use I'd be to you."

"You're a grown woman," he pointed out, tongue-in-cheek.

She looked at him, wide-eyed. "You mean I could be in Buenos Aires by tomorrow morning?"

"In my bed is more what I had in mind."

"Really?" She tried to sound amused, sophisticated, but just the thought of being in bed with him made her voice come out oddly squeaky. "And that's your idea of protection?"

"Well, if you want protection from *me*, you need to look no further than my housekeeper."

It sounded so English that Lisa exclaimed in surprise, "You have a housekeeper?"

"Mrs Kirk... She's the soul of propriety. The daughter

of a Scottish minister, at one time the wife of a parson, now a respectable widow.''

He laughed suddenly. ''You think I'm pulling your leg again?''

''It did cross my mind.''

''Well, I'm not. It's all quite true. When I first engaged her I was frightened to death of her.'' Humorously he added, ''To tell you the truth, I still am.''

Lisa gave a little gurgle of laughter.

''She rules my apartment with a rod of iron.''

Which brought them back to practicalities. ''Where is your apartment?'' she asked.

Casually he answered, ''Fifth Avenue, overlooking Central Park.''

Where else? she thought drily. Mark's apartment was uptown, but with a much less prestigious address.

While they'd been talking they had come through the Queens Midtown Tunnel beneath the East River and were now in the glass, steel and concrete canyons of Manhattan. The sun had set, and an indigo dusk, spangled with myriad, many-coloured lights, was draping the city in a bejewelled evening cloak.

Any other time Lisa would have been wholly entranced, but now only part of her attention was given to the spectacular skyscrapers and teeming traffic, the crowded sidewalks, the hubbub and dazzle that was New York by night. The other part was absorbed by her companion and the situation she found herself in.

Thorn Landers was disturbing in more ways than one. On discovering who he was, she had half expected an arrogant, humourless money man with an inflated opinion of himself. But though there was arrogance in the tilt of that dark head he was also charming, intelligent and exceedingly attractive.

Power and great wealth could give a man spurious sex appeal, but there was nothing phoney about *his* magnetism.

And he was kind. Beneath the surface teasing he seemed to be genuinely concerned about her; otherwise why bother to meet her and take her back to his apartment? Yet, having said all that, Lisa was uneasily aware of undercurrents, of *something* she didn't understand—

"This is Fifth Avenue." His voice broke into her thoughts. Staring out of the window at the famous thoroughfare, she saw galleries and museums scattered amongst big-name shops and luxury apartment buildings.

As they drew level with the tall and spectacular Fitzgerald building the Mercedes turned into a private forecourt, and an electronically controlled barrier across the entrance to an underground car park lifted to let them through.

He stopped the car in a yellow-numbered parking bay and came round to help her out. They were right next to a row of elevators and a concrete and glass security booth.

A thick-set man with a navy blue uniform, a peaked cap and a tough but pleasant face appeared and said in a gravelly voice, "Evening, Mr Landers."

"Evening, Joe. This is Miss Hayward... She's going to be my guest for a few weeks."

Lisa gave Joe a wide, friendly smile.

"Evening, miss." He beamed back approvingly. Pretty as a picture, this one, with a smile that made you feel as though the sun was shining, he thought. And no side to her...not like some of the others.

Tossing the car keys across, Thorn asked, "Get Pete to bring up the luggage, will you?"

"Sure thing."

His hand at her waist, making her whole body tingle as though in anticipation, Thorn led Lisa to his private elevator. He stood so close that her heart began to thump.

"Joe reminds me of William Bendix," she remarked a shade breathlessly as they sped smoothly up to the top floor.

Looking amused, Thorn said, "Me too... But I'm surprised you've even *heard* of William Bendix."

"Mrs Bartholomew, the lady I helped to take care of, was fond of watching old films," Lisa explained as they came to a stop and the doors slid open.

The entrance lobby was pale marble, with several classical statues, a crystal chandelier, and an elegant marble staircase curving downwards. So this was how the other half lived!

Opposite the staircase was a white and gilt door which swung open in obedience to Thorn's electronic key. Trying not to feel overawed, she allowed herself to be ushered across a spacious hall and into the main living area.

It was both beautiful and extensive, the decor basically white, splashed with vibrant touches of colour. Furnished simply but comfortably, with the minimum of modern pieces, it was the home of a man who liked his living to be gracious and uncluttered.

As Lisa looked around a woman appeared. Scrawny, severe-looking, with short iron-grey hair ruffled into a cockscomb and steel-rimmed glasses, she was incongruously dressed in baggy green and purple trousers, a sweatshirt and sneakers.

"Ah, Mrs Kirk..." Thorn said while Lisa did her best not to goggle. She could almost have sworn that his voice trembled with laughter, but when he turned to make the introduction he was straight-faced.

"How do you do?" Lisa murmured politely.

The housekeeper's dark eyes, bright as a robin's, surveyed her unsmilingly.

Far from comfortable, Lisa said apologetically, "I'm afraid my being here will make a lot of extra work for you."

It seemed that she'd passed some kind of test. The woman's stern face relaxed as she exclaimed, "Och, away with you!" Then, with a twinkle, she added, "And what has the man been telling you? That I'm a dragon, no doubt."

Deciding on diplomacy, Lisa answered, "He said you were the soul of propriety."

"Did he now?" Mrs Kirk eyed Thorn suspiciously. "Well, I'll be away to my bed. I've left a wee bite of supper for the lassie."

As the housekeeper disappeared towards her own quarters Lisa, feeling reassured, asked, "Has she been with you long?"

"Since her husband died about ten years ago. She's been in the States for over fifteen years."

"She still has a Scottish accent—" A buzzer cut through Lisa's words, heralding the arrival of her luggage.

When Pete, a pasty, red-headed youth, had been directed where to put the cases and had departed, pocketing a generous tip, Thorn led the way through to the kitchen.

It was large and airy, a designer's dream, tiled in navy blue and white, with a horseshoe-shaped breakfast-bar and bench. There was a delicious aroma of coffee, and Mrs Kirk's "wee bite of supper' would have amply fed a dozen.

Looking at the repast, Lisa admitted, "I'm thirsty, but not at all hungry."

"Too many of those plastic trays?" Thorn suggested quizzically.

Laughing, she agreed, "I wouldn't be a bit surprised."

"Though it's more likely to be the time-difference. Unless you're used to partying at three o'clock in the morning?"

She shook her head. Apart from tending old Mrs Bartholomew all she'd ever done at that time was sleep.

An occasional all-night party would certainly have enlivened her existence, she thought wistfully.

Aloud, she said, "I feel terribly guilty about all that food."

"There's no need to. It won't be wasted. First thing tomorrow morning Mrs Kirk will pack it up and take it to the East Side Mission, to feed the homeless.

"Now, what would you like to drink? Something long and cold—fruit juice or home-made lemonade perhaps...?" Being offered lemonade made her feel like a schoolgirl. "Coffee might keep you awake."

She was so tired that a brass band playing fortissimo in the same room was unlikely to do that. "Coffee sounds nice," she said defiantly.

Shrugging, Thorn lifted the glass jug and poured steaming black liquid into a couple of thick mugs, which were as incongruous in this designer kitchen as Mrs Kirk's sweatshirt and sneakers had been in the elegant lounge.

As he handed Lisa's to her their fingers touched. She jumped as though she'd received an electric shock. His green eyes smiled into hers, faintly mocking. "Hot?"

"Yes." She slid onto the bench and immediately wished she hadn't. If Thorn sat down on the end she would be trapped.

But though he watched her with a faintly brooding expression on his lean dark face he made no effort to join her, drinking his coffee standing where he was.

After a moment he broke the silence to query kindly, "How old are you, Lisa—eighteen, nineteen?"

Though disturbed by the effect he had on her, and knowing she *ought* to feel safer, she felt obscurely annoyed when he treated her like a child. Lifting her chin, she replied spiritedly, "I'll soon be twenty-one. How old are you?"

A gleam of amusement in those extraordinary eyes, he answered, "Nearly thirty-three."

"That old!" she mocked. "Even so, I can't think of you as a father-figure."

His voice silky, he informed her, "I wasn't intending that you should. The *last* thing I want to be to you is a father."

Excitement mingled with alarm as something predatory in his look made a shiver like a cold breath of wind run over her skin.

He saw that slight movement and his expression changed. His face now holding only casual interest, he went on, "You told me earlier that you left the States when you were three?"

"Yes. After my parents' marriage finally broke up my mother took me back to England."

"She was British?"

Lisa nodded. "She was born and bred in Sussex and felt she had her roots there...though by that time my grand-parents were both dead."

"Why didn't she take Mark?"

"She wanted to, but my father only agreed to a divorce on condition that she left his son with him. At first she refused. Then they decided, as Mark was almost fourteen, to ask him. He chose to stay with his father."

"Was it an amicable parting?"

"No. There was a great deal of bitterness on both sides. Mother did her best to keep in touch with Mark, but though she wrote regularly until she died she never got a single reply.

"I only found out afterwards that all her letters had been destroyed unopened..." Lisa's voice shook slightly and her eyes filled with tears. She looked away, trying not to blink.

"You and your mother were close?"

"Very."

As though giving her time to collect herself Thorn re-filled both coffee-mugs before saying, "Go on."

Swallowing hard, she obeyed. "I only heard from Mark after our father's death... By a strange coincidence both our parents died within a few weeks of each other—Father from a heart attack, Mother in a road accident."

Thorn's level black brows drew together in a frown. "After nearly eighteen years of not caring, what made him get in touch with you then?"

"But he *did* care." The gladness showed in Lisa's expressive face. "He said he'd always felt guilty about not keeping in touch, but he hadn't wanted to go against Father's wishes."

A sharp edge to his voice, Thorn demanded, "If he'd been so influenced by his father that you were virtually strangers, why did he want you to come over here?"

Somewhat awkwardly, she answered, "I don't really know, but it seemed to bother him that I'd been left nothing in Father's will—though I certainly hadn't expected anything. He asked me about my circumstances..."

"And?"

"I told him."

"Tell me."

Somewhat unwillingly she complied. "I was in the position of having neither a home nor a job."

"How come?"

"When Mother took me back to England, as well as a job she needed somewhere for us to live. She found a post as housekeeper-companion to an elderly lady who didn't mind having a young child about the house.

"It was a big old place, and by the time I left school Mrs Bartholomew was practically bedridden and needed a lot of care, so instead of getting a job I helped to look after her and run the house."

Thorn was watching her closely, his dark face shuttered, hiding his thoughts.

"Shortly after my mother's accident poor Mrs

Bartholomew had a stroke. She needed round-the-clock nursing, so her relatives arranged to have her taken care of in a private nursing home and put the house up for sale.''

''So when Mark knew how things stood he asked you to come over here?''

''Yes.''

''And you agreed.''

Nettled by his tone, sensing criticism, Lisa said sharply, ''I wasn't looking for a hand-out. He offered to find me a job and somewhere to live, that's all. There wasn't a lot to keep me in England.''

Quite the reverse in fact, and, feeling as though she'd reached a dead end in her life, she'd jumped at the chance to make a new and exciting start.

The green eyes were hooded. ''No boyfriend?''

There had been several, but none of them special until Ian had come along. She'd been quietly happy with him, hopeful that they could make a future together, until he'd left her for a sexy blonde named Janine.

Coolly she answered, ''No one I couldn't bear to leave.''

''No kith and kin?''

''One or two friends. But Mark's the only close relative I have in the world.''

And he hadn't even been there to meet her.

Thorn had admitted responsibility for that, however, so she mustn't blame Mark... But surely he could have scrawled her a few lines before he left...?

''He didn't leave a note for me?''

''A note?'' Just for a moment Thorn looked startled. ''Were you expecting one?''

''Not *expecting* exactly, but I just thought he might have...'' The words tailed off.

''So far as I'm aware he didn't leave a note. It must have slipped his mind in the last-minute rush.''

Once again she got the strange impression that Thorn was lying, hiding something.

But patently that was nonsense. All these bizarre thoughts and fancies could probably be put down to jet lag, which was causing her tired mind to play tricks.

Yet it was funny that Mark hadn't left her even a scribbled note. She would have expected him to...

CHAPTER TWO

WATCHING Lisa's expressive face, Thorn asked quickly, "More coffee?" She shook her head. "Then do you want to drop straight into bed, or shall I show you the rest of the penthouse?"

Suddenly feeling more lively—perhaps it was the coffee—she said, "I'd like to see the rest."

Apart from Mrs Kirk's quarters and the rooms she'd already seen there were three quietly luxurious bedrooms with *en suite* bathrooms, a long dining-room, a book-lined study-cum-office and a large, well-equipped gym.

"No swimming pool?" she teased.

"There's one in the basement. I swim every morning before breakfast."

No wonder he looked so fit, she thought.

In the living-room, as in the kitchen, one entire wall was made of long panels of smoked glass that slid aside to give access to a patio and roof garden.

The night air was cool and, despite the traffic fumes, oddly fresh. There were huge tubs of flowers and leafy trees, and somewhere close at hand Lisa could hear the musical splash of a fountain.

Peering through a screen of scented shrubs, she saw a bronze statuette of a laughing merchild riding the crest of a wave on the back of a dolphin, while water poured round them into a large, shell-shaped basin. It had such a joyous feeling of life and movement that she almost expected the pair to disappear into the swirling water. She gave a delighted exclamation.

"You like my Peter Sebastian?"

Lifting a glowing face to her companion, she said with truth, "It's *exquisite*."

"So are you." He sounded as if he meant it.

Although she knew quite well that she was nothing of the kind, she was still thrilled by the compliment. Her heart suddenly racing, she moved to the stone balustrade to look across the city.

Thorn followed and stood by her side, so near that she could feel the warmth of his body and smell the faint tang of his aftershave. After a second or two she became nerve-rackingly aware that he was staring not at the scene spread before him but at *her*.

The view over Central Park and night-time Manhattan was spectacular but, conscious only of the man by her side, Lisa was blind to the magic of it.

His will, so much stronger than hers, seemed intent on drawing her gaze. For a while she struggled against it, oddly convinced that if she so much as glanced at him she would be lost.

"Lisa..." He spoke her name softly.

As though there was no help for it she turned her head and looked into that dark face. Instantly she was caught and held, spellbound by the austere yet sensual line of his mouth, the arrogant tilt of his black head, his coolly ironic green eyes and sheer male magnetism.

He smiled—a little, satisfied smile—then asked, "You must be ready for bed?"

The casual words released her from the spell.

"Yes, I..." She tore her gaze away.

"Come along, then." He escorted her inside and to the beautiful green and white room where the weedy youth had put her cases. At the door, he held out his hand. Surprised by the formal gesture, she put hers into it. Then, with cool deliberation, Thorn used the hand he was holding to draw her, unprotesting, into his arms.

Using a single finger, he tipped her face up to his and covered her mouth with his own. Though his kiss was experimental there was nothing tentative about it, and that light but sure touch made the world tilt on its axis.

A moment later, dazed and breathless, she was free. He said a soft, "Goodnight, Lisa," and was gone.

She went into her room and, like someone in a dream, unpacked her nightclothes and toilet things, and prepared for bed in the sumptuous bathroom. The face gazing back at her from the angled mirror was flushed; the lambent hazel eyes looked almost intoxicated.

How was it that up until now many a more passionate embrace had left her senses only pleasantly stirred, while just the memory of Thorn's lips feathering across hers made her feel as though she'd jumped out of a plane at ten thousand feet without a parachute?

Having climbed into the big, luxurious bed, Lisa switched out the lamp and settled herself. Expecting to fall asleep as soon as her eyelids closed and darkness enfolded her, instead she found disturbing thoughts and questions rising up and fluttering like pale moths through her mind.

Why had Thorn Landers kissed her?

Though his kiss had made her lose her equilibrium, somehow her subconscious had registered a chilling fact. There had been something cool and *calculated* about it, as though he'd kissed her not because he'd felt the urge to but because he'd wished to judge her reaction.

But, if he hadn't really *wanted* to kiss her, what had been the point?

A man like him wouldn't be short of women to kiss. He'd told her that he had no current mistress, but she refused to believe that that situation wasn't of his determining.

Women would be falling over themselves to be with him in whatever capacity he chose. And not only because he was wealthy and powerful. If he hadn't had a cent she was sure the response would have been the same. His stunning looks and that smouldering sex appeal, overlaid with a certain cool aloofness, were an irresistible combination.

It was a combination that had already bewitched her and the prospect of spending at least the next three weeks under his roof generated a mixture of excitement and danger within her.

But there was no likelihood of her becoming seriously involved, she told herself, determinedly ignoring a feeling that might have been regret. Potent though it was, the spell he'd unwittingly cast was bound to be short-lived.

Unwittingly? She wasn't so sure. Perhaps it *was* deliberate. Maybe, thinking her to be naïve and green, he'd decided to amuse himself, have some fun with her.

A reckless desire to live dangerously for once, to play with fire, suggested that it could be fun for them both. For a short while.

When these three weeks or so were over she was unlikely ever to see him again. They were bound to move in quite different circles, lead totally different lives.

It was a curiously depressing thought.

She did her best to push it away and concentrate on the more immediate future, with its promise of excitement and pleasure…

Lisa surfaced slowly, and stretched. Brushing away the clinging cobwebs of sleep, she opened her eyes to find daylight filtering through the blinds.

The room was a strange one and for a moment or two she was completely disorientated. Then recollection came flooding back, bringing a tidal wave of exhilaration in its wake.

For whatever reason, Thorn Landers had kissed her, and nothing would ever be quite the same again. Just knowing that he was in the world made it a thrilling place.

And out there lay the Big Apple and the start of a new life. Thanks to Mark.

For the first time since her mother's death the dark shadow lifted wholly from her spirit and she felt a quick jubilation, a rush of impatience and enthusiasm to begin *living*.

Tumbling out of bed, she partially opened the vertical slats to let bright sunlight make tiger-stripes across the dark green duvet and ivory carpet. Peering at the watch she'd adjusted to New York time on the plane, she saw that it was nearly half past one.

Still, it was no wonder. After the first few hours of exhausted sleep she had lain awake, her brain active, a victim to the time-change, until the early hours of the morning, when she had dropped off again.

Padding about in her bare feet, she unpacked quickly and efficiently, stowing her small number of off-the-peg clothes in the luxurious walk-in wardrobes with a wry grin.

When she'd showered she dressed in a mutlicoloured button-through dress that was as charming as it was cheap, and took her riot of glossy brown curls up into a pony-tail before venturing forth. It was Friday, she realised, so Thorn would almost certainly be at work.

Bearing out that conclusion, the apartment appeared to be silent and deserted; then, very faintly, Lisa heard the sound of music and canned laughter.

She found Mrs Kirk in the kitchen, dressed in a canary-yellow tracksuit, one eye on a television game show while she finished rolling pizza bases.

''So there you are, lassie!'' She turned off the set. ''Help yourself to fruit juice or coffee and I'll get you something to eat. Will pastrami on rye do you?''

''Yes, thank you,'' Lisa replied politely, without the faintest idea what pastrami on rye was, but eager for new experiences. ''I'm sorry I slept so late,'' she added, pouring a glass of freshly squeezed orange juice and taking it over to the breakfast-bar. ''It must be a nuisance for you.''

''Och, away with you. Mr Landers told me to let you lie.''

''He's working?''

Bustling about with a frying-pan and a pile of pink, wafer-thin sliced meat she'd taken from the huge fridge, the housekeeper said cheerfully, ''He went to his office first thing, but now you're up I'll give him a call.''

''Oh, no, please don't disturb him on my account. I can easily look around on my—''

''They were my orders,'' Mrs Kirk broke in firmly. ''He doesn't want you to go wandering about on your own until you've got a bit more streetwise.''

''But that's ridiculous,'' Lisa protested, suddenly feeling like a prisoner. ''What possible harm could I come to on Fifth Avenue?''

Mrs Kirk shrugged bony shoulders. ''He feels responsible for you.'' Putting a slice of dark-seeded bread onto a plate, she piled the hot meat onto it and added a second slice to make a sandwich. ''There.''

It took two hands to pick it up and smelled so delicious that it made Lisa's mouth water. ''That's scrumptious!'' she exclaimed after the first bite. Then, at the woman's nod of approval, she asked, ''What *is* pastrami exactly?''

''Seasoned smoked beef. Some people eat it as it comes, but I've always preferred it hot myself...''

While Lisa tucked in with a healthy appetite the housekeeper disappeared, presumably to ring Thorn.

Her simple lunch finished, Lisa had just poured herself

a coffee when Mrs Kirk returned. Sliding one of the smoked-glass panels aside, the older woman observed, "There's a lounger in the garden if you'd like to take your coffee outside."

Smiling her thanks, Lisa went out onto the terrace. It was sunny and felt baking hot after the coolness of the air-conditioned apartment. As she stretched out in the partial shade of a pale blue ringed umbrella, the housekeeper added, "Mr Landers will be home directly…"

New York might have had a reputation for being a violent city, with more than its fair share of muggers, but surely thousands of nice, ordinary people lived and worked and played here quite safely? Lisa thought with a touch of exasperation, watching a white cotton-wool cloud slowly change shape as it moved across the lapis lazuli-coloured sky.

Her clothes weren't expensive, to say the least. She hadn't a gold watch, a designer handbag or a camera to her name, no diamonds or pearls on display, so why on earth did Thorn feel it necessary to leave his work and escort her as though she were a child?

Still, the prospect of having him with her certainly wasn't an unwelcome one. Though in many ways his presence disturbed her, it also challenged and excited her, heightening her senses and making all her perceptions jewel-bright…

When she opened her eyes Thorn was there by her side. His jacket dangling from one finger, the knot in his tie loosened, he was standing looking down at her, tall and dark and *threatening*—now what on earth had put *that* word into her mind?—brilliant eyes narrowed against the sun.

"I must have dropped off." She was flustered. "The last thing I remember was watching a fluffy white cloud change from a rabbit into a poodle…" And now she was babbling!

Looking amused, he agreed, "Soporific things, clouds." Sitting down by her side, his hip touching hers, he queried, "Still tired?"

As the bright sunlight slanted across his face she saw that his eyes—handsome, *fascinating* eyes—had tiny pin-points of gold swimming in their dark green depths...

"Not really. It must be the warmth." Though her lungs seemed deprived of air and her heart felt as though it was on a trampoline, somehow she managed to keep her voice steady.

"Well, if you prefer to just take it easy rather than go out...?"

"Oh, no!" she exclaimed. "I can't *wait* to get to know New York."

"Any particular part?"

"The Bronx, Staten Island, Brooklyn, but, most of all, Manhattan and Central Park..."

Laughing, he stood up, and, holding out a lean, tanned hand, hauled her to her feet. "Well, as the only way to see Manhattan properly is on foot, we'd better get started... And, if you're in agreement, I think that with so much to see it makes more sense to get a general picture first and do the in-depth stuff later."

She nodded happily.

Glancing down at her high heels, he added, "I suggest you put on some comfortable shoes and grab a light jacket to protect you from the sun, while I get rid of this suit and tie."

A few minutes later they were going down in the elevator. Thorn, seeming even taller, had changed into casual trousers and an open-necked fawn shirt. The sleeves had been pushed up to show tanned, muscular arms, lightly sprinkled with dark hair. He looked cool and dynamic and disturbingly attractive.

After glancing with approval at her flat-heeled white sandals he remarked, "Ideal."

"It was these or nothing," she admitted. "I don't buy many flat shoes. I'm not tall enough."

"Does that worry you?"

"I don't let it. I just pretend I'm as I'd like to be."

"And how's that?"

"Five foot eight, with long, slim legs, blue eyes and smooth blonde hair," she answered promptly. But somehow the thought of Janine didn't bother her any more.

Hooking a finger in one of her curls, he straightened it and let it spring back. "Then these are natural?"

"Unfortunately."

Shaking his head, he said, "I much prefer you as you are. Long-legged, smooth-haired blondes are a dime a dozen."

She knew he was probably joshing, but all the same his words gave her a warm glow.

He stopped the elevator in the main lobby, and they walked across what seemed like acres of polished marble to the imposing glass doors where a uniformed security guard hovered.

They were strolling down Fifth Avenue, past expensive shops and elegant apartment buildings, when a sudden thought made Lisa glance at her companion and ask, "Is Mark's apartment far from here?"

"A mile or so." Thorn's answer was casual, but she could have sworn that for some reason the question had made him wary. "Why do you ask?"

"I just thought I'd like to see where he lives."

"Then I'll show you," he promised swiftly. "But not today. I've other things planned. To start with, a drive through Central Park."

To her surprise and pleasure it proved to be in one of the open horse-drawn carriages drawn up outside the Plaza

Hotel. As soon as they were seated the top-hatted driver clicked to his rosette-bedecked horse, and they went bowling merrily through one of the most beautiful and best known parks in the world.

Lisa looked at everything with shining eyes, loving the way it seemed to be bursting with life and vitality, with people walking, cycling, picnicking, playing games or just lazing on the grass enjoying the sunshine.

"I wonder if Mark ever comes here?" She spoke her thoughts aloud. "I really know so little about him—what kind of person he is, what his pastimes are. I still have no idea what he looks like..." She glanced at her companion.

His face strongly set, Thorn answered the appeal in her glance. "He's about my height, well built, with fair hair and brown eyes. Women seem to find him quite irresistible."

His words held a bite that surprised her. Anger? Bitterness? Resentment? No, surely not. She must be reading him wrongly. A man like Thorn Landers wouldn't need to be jealous of *anyone*.

But certainly there seemed to be no love lost between him and Mark. At the airport he'd said they were business colleagues rather than friends... Perhaps they were rivals? In more ways than one?

She was about to ask just how well he knew Mark when, abruptly changing the subject, Thorn began to tell her about Central Park's zoo and its many other attractions... "There's horse-riding and open-air concerts and, in the winter, tobogganing and skating on the lake..."

When the drive was over and he had helped her down they headed south again, pausing outside Trump Tower to glance into the lavish atrium with its pink marble surfaces, cascading waterfall and luxuriant greenery.

Turning to resume their walk, they came face to face with a striking, well-dressed brunette. Her vivid young beauty was spoilt by too much make-up and a discontented, petulant expression.

"Thorn, darling!" she exclaimed. "How lovely to see you." The petulance disappeared, to be replaced by a look so full of longing, of sexual craving that it made Lisa uncomfortable.

"Carole…" He acknowledged the girl—for she was little more—with a coolness that to anyone less blindly besotted would have been off-putting.

After a quick, envious glance at Lisa she clutched at his arm, her long, plum-coloured nails curving against his tanned skin. "I can't tell you how much I've missed you… You knew I was back; I was hoping you'd ring me."

"I've been very busy," he said smoothly.

She pouted. "Too busy to return my calls even…" When he said nothing she rushed on, "You will come to the party Daddy's giving for my birthday, won't you? Oh, you *must*; it won't be the same without you…"

The girl's desperate eagerness was only too evident. "It's in six weeks' time at the Waldorf. Everyone will expect you to be there. Please say you'll try…"

His dark face sardonic, Thorn said, "I'll try. Now if you'll excuse us…" A hand at Lisa's waist, he shepherded her away. She was conscious of Carole's hungry gaze following them.

He had made no effort to introduce the two women, and his haste to end the encounter had been barely within the bounds of politeness. Not that Lisa had wanted to linger. His studied indifference in the face of the girl's desperation had made the little incident far from pleasant.

She shivered. She would hate him to look at *her* with that mixture of uninterest and cool disdain.

As though sensing her discomfort, he apologised. "I'm sorry about that. She's just a silly, spoilt child."

Obscurely angered by that casual dismissal, Lisa said, "She's obviously in love with you."

"Infatuated," he corrected her.

"I felt sorry for her."

"You've no need to."

"You could have been—" Lisa bit her tongue.

"Kinder?"

"Yes."

"Ever heard of being cruel to be kind?" he asked curtly. "Sometimes it's the only way."

Biting her lip, dismayed that they were quarrelling, clouding what should have been a wonderful day, she muttered, "I'm sorry... It's really none of my business if you want to end the relationship."

"There is no *relationship* to end..." Bringing them both to an abrupt halt beneath the blue and gold awning of an expensive boutique, he took her upper arms in a grip that could hardly have been called gentle.

She thought for a moment that he was going to shake her. But, apparently resisting the temptation, he held her gaze and went on with dangerous softness, "Rather than feeling sorry for Carole you should spare a thought for me. I never gave her the slightest encouragement—just the opposite in fact—yet she pestered me for months..."

"I'm sorry," Lisa said helplessly. "I didn't realise."

But he hadn't finished. "All her life Carole's father has bought her everything she's ever wanted. He even tried to buy me. When he found he couldn't he took my advice and sent her to Europe for six months... Unfortunately it doesn't seem to have had the desired effect."

"I'm sorry," Lisa repeated.

Releasing her, he gave a short, sharp sigh. "Now suppose we forget the whole thing and get on with our sight-seeing?"

She was only too glad to agree.

It was hot and dusty but, apart from an occasional taxi ride, they walked for hours, zigzagging from St Pat's on Fifty-first and Fifth, right down to Battery Park, with its fine view across the bay to the Statue of Liberty.

As well as being an interesting, stimulating companion with a good, often dry sense of humour, Thorn proved to be an excellent guide, displaying a wide and intimate knowledge of Manhattan.

The Rockefeller Center, the Empire State Building, Washington Square Park, the hub of trendy Greenwich Village, SoHo, with its fascinating cast-iron buildings, Chinatown, full of exotic shops and pagoda-topped telephone kiosks, colourful Little Italy and the world-famous Wall Street were no longer just names to Lisa but places she'd actually seen with her own eyes and knew about.

She was ecstatic, and made no attempt to conceal it, giving an impulsive little skip of pure joy. If Thorn thought her unsophisticated, so what? But perhaps her pleasure was infectious, because he seemed to be enjoying everything as much as she was.

On the whole his disturbing proximity had been easier to cope with than she might have expected. If a smiling glance or the light touch of his hand when he wanted to draw her attention to something made her lose both her breath and the thread of what he was saying, hopefully she was managing to hide it.

Heading up Broadway, which Lisa was surprised to find ran the entire length of Manhattan, they stopped in a shady outdoor café to have a glass of iced soda water.

Watching people, red-faced and perspiring, walking past, Thorn remarked, "Even when the sun goes down it's unlikely to get much cooler."

"I don't mind," she told him cheerfully. "Luckily I've always been able to stand heat."

"Not exhausted yet?"

She shook her head.

"Then you must see uptown Broadway and Times Square by night... But before we go much further I suggest we eat. Do you like spaghetti?"

"I adore any kind of pasta." There was no doubt about her enthusiasm.

"Thank God you're not one of those women who live on lettuce leaves." He spoke with such fervour that Lisa found herself wondering if his last lady-friend *had* been.

Returning through Little Italy, they stopped at Mamma Mia's, a small basement restaurant with red-checked tablecloths and candles stuck in raffia-encased Chianti bottles.

The fat proprietress greeted Thorn like an old friend and produced plates of steaming spaghetti and a bottle of red wine, while a hook-nosed man with a drooping moustache played a guitar and serenaded the customers.

It was a lively, romantic place, and though she agreed with Thorn that it was stereotyped Lisa loved it and said so. He surprised her by saying, "So do I. I come here when I want a complete change from my usual haunts."

By the time they had finished their espresso it was dark outside and, as he'd forecast, still hot and sticky. He got a cab to drop them in the heart of the theatre district.

After an extended tour on foot, the bright lights and flashing neon signs even more spectacular and garish than Lisa had expected, they stopped for a drink in one of the quieter bars.

When she sat down, fatigue suddenly caught up with her, swallowing her like an avalanche, but it was purely physical; her mind was still leaping.

Thorn, she noted with rueful admiration, not only looked alert but cool and fresh enough to run a marathon.

Smiling at her, he asked, "What would you like?"

Trying to hide the fact that she was at a loss, she queried, "What are you having?"

"Bourbon on the rocks."

"That sounds fine," she said airily.

"I wouldn't recommend it for a novice drinker..."

After a day of wonderful companionship, a day of being on an equal footing, there he was treating her like a child again!

Thinking, if he offers me lemonade I'll scream, Lisa demanded spiritedly, "What makes you so sure I'm a novice?"

Shrugging slightly, he said, "Then bourbon it is."

A cautious sip of the dark amber liquid convinced her that she'd have been better off with lemonade, but, determined not to admit it, she assumed an air of nonchalance and waited for the melting ice to weaken the strong spirit.

Her strategy didn't fool him for a moment. Eyes gleaming, he asked, "What do you think of it compared to Scotch?"

Refusing to rise to the bait, she sought to divert him. "Just then you sounded quite English. Have you spent much time in the UK?"

"I was educated there."

Wanting to know more about him, she asked, "Have you British ancestry?"

"My grandfather came from the Midlands. After emigrating to the States and making quite a bit of money he finally settled in the East and started to build a business empire which included shipping, real estate and industry.

"But though he married and lived here quite happily he still thought Britain's universities were the best in the world, so my father, who was an only child, was sent to Oxford to be educated."

"And you followed in his footsteps, a kind of family tradition in the making? Did your brother go too, or were *you* an only child?"

The innocent question had a shattering effect. She saw

him freeze, and his dark face grew set and bleak while a muscle jumped in his jaw as though his teeth were tightly clenched. After a moment he answered shortly, "No. I had a sister."

Noticing the past tense, and scenting a tragedy, Lisa was searching desperately for something to say to change the subject when he remarked abruptly, "You must be tired. We'd better be getting home."

On the sidewalk, he hailed a cab, and after giving its driver the address stayed silent and withdrawn while they inched their way through the heavy evening traffic to Fifth Avenue.

By the time he'd helped Lisa out and paid the cabbie, however, to her great relief the tautness had gone from his face and he seemed to be himself again.

"I can't thank you enough," she said when he'd let them into what appeared to be a deserted apartment. "I've had a marvellous time."

"So have I." He sounded as if he meant it.

Catching her surprised glance, he admitted a shade wryly, "Just lately I've found myself weary of blasé women who are only interested in what they look like— women who have lost the ability to just be themselves and enjoy life."

His fingers brushing her neck, so that her heart missed a beat, he slipped the jacket from her shoulders and placed it over the back of a chair before asking, "What would you like for a nightcap?"

She didn't really want anything, but the desire to stay with him a little longer proved too great. "Whatever you're having," she said recklessly, adding more sedately, "Then a cool shower before bed."

"Rather than a cool shower, I've a better idea. Just a minute…" He vanished to the kitchen to return a few moments later carrying a round tray loaded with a bottle of iced champagne, a jug of orange juice and two glasses.

Balancing the tray on one palm with the dexterity of a waiter, he said, "Come with me," and, taking her hand, led her, weak-kneed, through the gym to a wall of glass at the end. "Be an angel and press that button for me."

Following the direction of his glance, Lisa saw a small button on the side-wall. When she put her finger on it the glass panels slid aside, letting in the velvety warmth of the night air.

To the right of the paved terrace was a low table and a couple of loungers, and in the middle a small, sunken pool, golden light reflecting off its inky black ripples. From it came the gentle splash and gurgle of moving water, while faint swirls of steam drifted upwards to hang like a gathering of genies in the still air before disappearing.

"A Jacuzzi," Thorn told her, stooping to put the tray on the table.

Realising what he had in mind, and suddenly going hot all over, Lisa said uneasily, "I know what a Jacuzzi is."

"But have you ever been in one?"

Loath to admit that she'd never even *seen* one, she answered as levelly as possible, "Well, no."

He disappeared inside the gym to return a second or two later with a couple of white towelling robes over his arm. "Then this is your chance. You'll find it very refreshing."

Breathless now, she said, "I…I didn't bring a costume." It wasn't exactly the truth. But there had never been much money for clothes and the only one she owned was old, and pulled across the bust. It dated from her schooldays when the fifth form had gone swimming at the local baths, and she shrank from the idea of him seeing her in that.

"My dear girl," he drawled, gently caustic, "the last thing you need is a costume. Just strip off and get in…"

During the day the pool would have been well shielded

by trees and bushes. At night, on a rooftop high above the city, with only the stars looking down, what did it matter anyway? But, of course, *that* wasn't the problem.

"Unless you're shy?" The words held a taunt, as though he thought it was prudish of her to be concerned about baring her body. While she tried to find some way out without sounding hopelessly stuffy and strait-laced he assured her, "I won't look, if you don't want me to."

Still she hesitated.

Pulling his shirt over his head, Thorn tossed it onto one of the loungers. "So what are we waiting for?" he asked, and Lisa saw the unmistakable glint of challenge in his eyes.

CHAPTER THREE

WELL, damn him! Lisa thought. She might just pick up the gauntlet.

As, giving herself no time for second thoughts, she began to undo the buttons on her dress, he smiled and asked mockingly, "To spare your blushes, shall I stare fixedly into the middle distance?"

"You can please your joyful," she snapped, the child-hood retaliation out before she could prevent it. Though she'd never flaunted her body she certainly wasn't ashamed of it!

Lifting her chin, she met his gaze defiantly while she finished unbuttoning her dress and allowed it to fall at her feet in a tumbled heap. A moment later her dainty undies followed.

For a second or two she stood quite still while the light from the gym shone on her pale, lissom figure. Dressed, she looked almost as slim as a boy. Undressed, she was a beautifully proportioned pocket Venus with firm, tip-tilted breasts, a tiny waist, curving hips and slender legs.

Thorn took a deep, audible breath and she saw surprise and admiration in his eyes before she turned away and walked sedately to the Jacuzzi.

One round to her, she thought triumphantly as she went down the steps into the bubbling pool. Or was it? Suddenly she wasn't so sure. She'd only done what he'd intended from the first.

A seat ran around the sides and she sat down, submerged up to her shoulders, her head against the wooden headrest.

High above her, stars gleamed in the indigo sky and a crescent moon hid modestly behind a wispy veil of white cloud. The heated water felt wonderful, kneading and massaging her tired muscles while a night breeze carrying the lemony scent of some shrub fanned her face. She gave a little murmur of pleasure.

"Glad you're enjoying it," Thorn remarked.

Glancing in his direction, she saw that he was pouring a mixture of champagne and orange juice into the glasses. He was stark naked.

Lisa had never seen a naked man in the flesh before. She wanted to look away and couldn't, her eyes fixed on him as though mesmerised.

Oh, but he was *beautiful*—lithe and graceful, with wide shoulders, narrow hips and long, straight legs, his skin gleaming like oiled silk in the light. His chest was muscular, roughened by a scattering of dark hair arrowing down to a flat stomach, while his back was smooth, the line of his spine elegant…

Suddenly he glanced up and caught her staring.

Heat which had nothing to do with the water temperature poured into her face. Somehow she dragged her gaze away.

He laughed softly. "Look all you want. I'm not shy."

As, throat dry, face burning, she stared blindly at nothing in particular he waded into the pool and sat down beside her.

"Here." He handed her a champagne glass. "Buck's Fizz… See how you like it."

"Mmm, delicious," she managed, sipping with her eyes closed, taut with awareness of that long, powerful body stretched beside her.

"Don't look so fraught," he chided, seeing her tension. "I'm not about to leap on you."

"I never thought you were," she muttered.

"Then relax and have fun."

But the whole situation made that impossible.

When the glass was empty he took it from her nerveless fingers and she heard him put it down on the side.

The water bubbled and swirled and eddied around her, the hot jets caressing her skin. It felt soothing, invigorating and sensual all at the same time, and gradually she relaxed and gave herself up to the sheer enjoyment of it.

He must have shifted position slightly because all at once his naked thigh was touching hers. She sat motionless, barely breathing. Wanting to move away. Not wanting to move away.

"Asleep?" he enquired softly. She felt his breath, warm and fresh, on her lips and her eyes flew open.

He smiled at her, his teeth very white in the darkness of his face. Then slowly, closing his own eyes so that his long lashes lay on his cheeks like black fans, he leaned towards her. His mouth felt for the shape of hers and he traced the outline with his tongue before using the tip of it to part her lips.

Instantly she was lost, defenceless, drowning in the sweetness of his kiss. It was the most wonderful, ecstatic feeling she had ever experienced, and she wanted it to go on for ever.

When he drew away she sighed and opened dazed eyes. His face was only inches from her own and she caught the unmistakable look of triumph on it.

That look was like a douche of icy water.

He saw her expression change and instantly the triumph was masked. But it was too late. The damage had been done. Struggling to her feet, she said thickly, "I'd like to get out now."

"Of course."

Following her up the steps, Thorn picked up one of the

big towelling robes and wrapped it around her before donning the other one himself.

"What we really need now," he suggested, "is a swim. At this time of night we'll have the pool to ourselves."

Tying the belt of the robe tight, she shook her head, scattering drops of water from the bedraggled ends of her pony-tail. "No, thanks." She used the deep towelling collar to rub her hair before gathering up her clothes and shoes. "I'll settle for a cool shower then bed."

Knowing he'd blown it, Thorn made no further attempt to persuade her but in silence accompanied her to her room.

Determined not to look as if she was lingering, she opened the door and with a distant, "goodnight," was about to disappear inside when he said casually,

"We'll have our swim tomorrow morning. I'll give you a knock about six."

"I...I told you, I haven't a costume...and I've no intention of going in without one."

"Heaven forbid," he said piously. "Well, goodnight, Lisa."

Safely in her room, the door closed behind her, she took herself to task while she showered and cleaned her teeth. What on earth had made her act so recklessly, so completely out of character?

In all probability it was the unaccustomed bourbon. In that case, whether it made her feel like a child or not, in future she would stick to lemonade. She'd behaved like an absolute fool, stripping off like that! Where was her pride, her dignity?

To hell with pride and dignity. Where was her *common sense*? If Thorn had kept on kissing her, if he'd turned on the heat, she could well have ended up in his bed.

The thought shook her rigid. It was one thing to toy with the idea of living dangerously, of playing with fire, but quite another to actually *do* it!

But she had never before realised how strong physical attraction could be.

Physical attraction, her foot! She was in love with the man.

So soon. So swiftly.

It wasn't the gentle, cautious kind of love, growing gradually from liking and respect to something deep and lasting, but a sudden impact that had sent her reeling like a sock on the jaw.

She had *wanted* his touch, *hungered* for his kiss. And it must have been quite obvious to a man of his experience.

Recalling his expression of cool disdain when he'd looked at the hapless Carole, Lisa groaned aloud. Even then she had known that she would hate him to look at *her* like that.

Well, she must give him no more cause to. No matter what it cost her, she must hide that helpless attraction and make sure that he had no further chance to make a fool of her. For that had obviously been what he'd intended. The look of triumph on his face had proved that. If his kiss had been genuine he would have acted quite differently.

This getting females to fall for him was obviously some kind of heartless game he played for his own amusement— a game he was good at. Well, now she knew the score he could count her out.

Climbing into bed, she thumped her pillow into submission, wishing it were Thorn's head. He was a cruel, arrogant swine. How *could* she have fallen in love with a man like that?

But she had.

So until she managed to kill that love she must keep it well hidden, otherwise she would be completely at his mercy. In the same boat as poor Carole…

If only she weren't trapped here with him for the next

three weeks. If only she didn't have to face him tomorrow...

Lisa gave herself a shake. All she needed to do was stay cool and calm and not let him get to her. She could blame the night's foolishness on the bourbon, and with a bit of luck he might believe her.

Once she could convince him that she was impervious to his attraction, he'd give up and write her off as a failure, leaving her pride intact. Then as soon as this enforced stay was over she need never see him again.

On that note of dismal optimism she fell asleep.

Lisa was awakened by a rapping on the door. ''Come on, sleepyhead,'' Thorn's voice called. ''It's almost a quarter after six.''

Muttering some very unladylike things beneath her breath, Lisa pushed back the lightweight duvet and struggled out of bed. Dragging on her dressing-gown, still flushed with sleep, her luxuriant mass of silky brown curls tumbling round her shoulders, she pulled open the door.

Freshly shaved, his black hair still wet from the shower, he was wearing flip-flops and a short towelling robe. Looking disturbingly handsome and sexy, his green eyes brilliant, he smiled down at her. ''Good morning.''

Despite everything her heart began to race with suffocating speed.

''Sleep well?'' he queried.

Making an effort, she answered politely, ''Very well, thank you. Did you?''

''Not as well as usual,'' he admitted ruefully.

Lying awake, his hands clasped behind his head, he'd thought about her standing naked beside the Jacuzzi, slim and delicate, yet surprisingly voluptuous.

But as well as the pleasure he'd felt at the sight of her

lovely body he'd remembered her spirit and courage, the look in her eyes of mingled misgiving and defiance, the reckless resolve that had been a response to his goading. Unexpectedly he'd found her interesting and intriguing, and if she hadn't been who she was...

Snapping off the thought like a dry twig, his face unconsciously hardening, he asked, "Ready for that swim?"

"I *told* you, I haven't got a costume."

"You have now." He handed her a small package. "It should be the right size. Hurry up and get changed. I'll give you five minutes." Before she could draw breath to argue he was gone.

In something of a twitter she opened the flat box, and from the folds of tissue paper took out a deceptively simple subtle gold and brown leopard-spotted bikini, complete with short matching jacket and stretched headband.

It was exactly her size. But where on earth had he got it from?

Though she knew quite well that she couldn't afford something so obviously expensive, curiosity made her try the ensemble on.

The briefs were slashed almost to the waist, making her legs look longer, and the plunging bra was strapless. But the expert cut meant that it was a perfect fit, and, glancing in the full-length mirror, she saw that the whole thing looked absolutely stunning.

She was still staring goggle-eyed at the exotic creature reflected there when a prolonged rapping told her that the five minutes were up. This time when she opened the door she saw that he was carrying a couple of towels over his arm.

"Good, you're ready," he greeted her. "Let's go."

She shook her head. "I can't...I can't wear this."

"You look sensational," he said with truth. "You've

changed from a kitten into a sleek and beautiful jungle cat.''

Trying to ignore the outrageous flattery, she informed him flatly, ''Designer stuff like this is right out of my price range.''

''It's already paid for.''

''Thank you,'' she said frostily, ''but I've no intention of letting you buy clothes for me.''

He shrugged those wide shoulders. ''If it bothers you I'll make sure your brother reimburses me.''

''Nor have I any intention of sponging off Mark.'' She would sooner wear her old costume, or not go at all.

If he'd shown the slightest sign of irritation or annoyance, or tried to force the issue, she might have won the battle. But instead, seeing the determined lines of her mouth and chin, he said reasonably, ''OK, so I admire you for that. But don't let's begin the day on a sour note... You can always pay me back when you start work.

''Besides,'' he went on plaintively, ''if I have to return it Joe will be disappointed.''

''Joe?'' she exclaimed, startled. ''What's Joe got to do with it?''

''His wife runs a small boutique. Before I went to bed last night I rang him up and told him what I wanted. When he came on duty at five-thirty this morning he brought me a selection to choose from.''

Tongue-in-cheek, Thorn added, ''So you see both Joe and his wife have gone to a great deal of trouble just so we could have a morning swim together... Unless, of course, you really don't want to?''

She tried to say she didn't, but oh, she *wanted* to. Common sense told her that it was unwise on more than one count, but still she was unable to make her lips frame the lie.

Reading her expressive face, he asked, "Then what are we waiting for?"

"I must just get my sandals."

When their elevator stopped at the pleasant recreational area, where bright umbrellas and flowering plants added to the ambience, she saw that they had the place to themselves, and though the pool-side snack bar was lit it was still closed, metal grilles in place.

The water looked inviting, turquoise blue and still as glass, reflecting back the lights.

Discarding his flip-flops and tossing the towels and his robe onto a convenient lounger, Thorn smiled at her. Wearing well-cut black swimming trunks that hugged his lean hips and emphasised the straight length of his legs, he looked tanned and fit and dangerously attractive, and she had a job to stop herself staring at him.

"Race you to the far end?" he suggested.

Though she knew she hadn't a chance in hell of even keeping up with him, she put her sandals and jacket beside the other things and followed him to the edge.

His eyes running appreciatively over her slender curves, he offered, "I'll give you a ten-second start."

It meant him watching her dive in, but she could hardly refuse. "How magnanimous of you," she said mockingly. Throwing her arms above her head and rising on tiptoe, she entered the water cleanly. It was cool and deliciously refreshing.

Knowing her dive had been quite creditable for someone so out of practice, she struck out for the shallow end of the Olympic-sized pool. Moments later Thorn surfaced beside her and kept pace with a lazy, effortless crawl. They finished together.

Shaking the water out of his eyes, he observed, "A dead heat, I believe."

"Come off it," she said inelegantly. "You could have won easily."

Green eyes smiling into hers, he murmured, "I always win at what I *want* to win at..."

Bothered and bewitched by that beguiling glance, she spoke without thinking. "Then you've never learnt how to be a good loser?"

He shook his head. "Show me a good loser and I'll show you a loser, period."

Momentarily repelled by such ruthlessness, Lisa turned hastily away and, changing to breast stroke, headed back.

By seven they had been joined by perhaps half a dozen people, dedicated swimmers doing measured lengths up and down the pool. They swam for a while longer until, obviously seeing that she was tiring, Thorn asked, "Had enough?"

"Yes," she admitted. "But you stay in if you want to."

He shook his head. "I'm ready for some coffee."

Reaching the side first, he heaved himself, dripping, onto the tiles and turned to offer his hands. A moment later she was hauled out like a child and wrapped in one of the white towels.

The snack bar was open now, and there was a delicious smell of coffee and pancakes and maple syrup. As soon as they had towelled themselves down and settled on a table, Thorn went to the counter and returned with two steaming mugs of coffee and a couple of freshly made doughnuts rolled in brown sugar.

"Mmm, that was delicious," Lisa said appreciatively a few minutes later, popping in the last piece and licking sugar from around her mouth. "And I really enjoyed the swim."

Watching her pink tongue travel over her lips, he asked idly, "As much as the Jacuzzi?"

As though she'd been dipped in hot water, her face turned scarlet.

Looking amused, he said, "There's no need to blush so furiously. I've seen a naked female body before."

Not *hers*, he hadn't.

"And it isn't a crime to let your hair down a little."

As far as she was concerned it had been a *lot*. "I don't remember too much about it," she lied desperately, wiping away a trickle of cold water that ran down her neck from her still wet curls. "Perhaps I should have taken your advice and not drunk the bourbon."

Ignoring the red herring, he pursued, "But you remember how you responded to my kiss?"

Giving up the pretence, she said shortly, "It won't happen again."

"You sound very positive."

"Oh, I am."

"Are you trying to tell me you didn't enjoy being kissed?"

"I'm trying to tell you I object to being made a fool of."

"Made a fool of?" he drawled.

So he was going to act dumb.

"*Why* did you kiss me?"

For a moment he looked both startled and annoyed, then, his face wiped clean of all expression save a faint wariness, he asked, "Why does any man kiss a woman?"

"You're a man, so you tell me."

His gaze lingering on her mouth, he said quizzically, "Usually because he can't resist the temptation."

"I don't think that was the reason in your case."

"You underrate your attraction, my lovely. And you were looking particularly seductive, if you remember—"

Goaded, Lisa snapped, "I remember the look of triumph on your face afterwards."

"That sounds almost like an accusation."

"It is."

The green eyes flashed. "Why? What kind of look did you expect? I enjoyed kissing you, and triumph is what any normal male would feel when a female he fancies responds to him."

The ground cut from under her feet, she gazed at him mutely.

"Would you have preferred me to look disappointed? Indifferent?"

"No," she conceded. "But I thought you were just... playing...trying to make me fall for you..."

His eyes narrowing, Thorn swore under his breath. This sweet little *ingénue* was more astute than he'd realised.

"...when to you it was only a game."

"You mean you could see me cutting notches on the bedpost?"

"Yes," she said defiantly, "that's exactly what I mean..." she saw something that might have been a flicker of relief cross his hard face "...except I don't think you were even serious enough to want to take—" Flushing a little, she broke off.

"Take you to bed?" he finished for her. "My sweet little innocent, any man with red blood in his veins would want to do that."

After a thoughtful pause, as though he'd been debating something tricky and had come to a decision, he reached across the white plastic table and took her hand, making her breath catch in her throat. "However, you are right about one thing. I *was* trying to make you fall for me..."

Perhaps, subconsciously, she'd only half believed it. Hearing him admit the truth shook her. As her hazel eyes widened he went on, "But you're wrong about everything else. It wasn't only a game and I wasn't just playing. I've never been more serious in my life."

So her lack of sophistication appealed to his jaded appetite and he wanted to make her his mistress. But for how long? A few weeks? A few months? And then what? Presumably she'd be thrown aside for the next woman to take his fancy.

He smiled into her eyes and, raising her hand to his lips, kissed the palm, folding her slim fingers inwards as though to hold the kiss, before releasing it.

Chills ran up and down her spine, and she saw his sharp eyes note the betraying little shiver. Realising afresh what danger she was in from her own feelings as well as his, and knowing she had to make a stand, she lifted her chin and informed him haughtily, "Well, I've no intention of having an affair with you."

"What makes you imagine I want an affair?"

Feeling incredibly foolish, she stammered, "I—I'm sorry, but I thought—"

"I want to marry you."

The wind taken completely out of her sails, she gaped at him.

"Your mouth's open," he told her silkily. "And it's giving me ideas I can't put into practice in a public place. So come on..." Gathering up their belongings, he seized her hand and hurried her to the bank of elevators.

As soon as the doors of the penthouse elevator slid to behind them he dropped the towels he was holding and, before Lisa could even catch her breath, pulled her forcefully to him.

Off balance, she clutched instinctively at his towelling robe. Loosely belted, it came apart, and suddenly she found the warmth of his muscular chest beneath her palms and his hair-roughened legs straddling and trapping the smoothness of hers.

For an endless, startled second she looked up at him, eyes wide and defenceless, lips parted. He smiled down at her recklessly, dynamically, with a smile that left her in no doubt that the heat was on. And that he wanted her to know it.

Then, with one hand in the small of her back, clamping her close, the other beneath her chin, holding her face up to his, Thorn began to kiss her with merciless expertise.

With the lower half of her body pressed to his, she felt the thrusting hardness of his male flesh against her yielding softness, and was aware of her own urgent anticipation like a liquid core of heat.

After a moment his hand moved from her chin to slip inside her flimsy jacket. The scanty bikini bra offered little protection from his marauding fingers, and in a trice his hand was cupped around her bare breast. When his thumb began to tease the nipple gently, her stomach tied itself in knots, and a delicious excitement engulfed her in mind-blowing waves.

It was like taking an out-of-control ride on a roller coaster, and by the time he lifted his dark head she was breathless and trembling, her legs so weak that she could hardly stand.

Easing her breasts back into the cup, he readjusted the material with long, lean fingers, the tip of his index finger lightly circling the unmistakable evidence of her arousal.

Then, smiling into her dazed face, he bent his head once more and licked the corner of her mouth, the sensual little caress affecting her almost as much as his kiss.

''Sugar...''

''What?'' she croaked.

''There's still a trace of sugar round your mouth.''

She became aware that the elevator had stopped and the doors were open. With no idea how long they had been standing there, she was profoundly thankful that the top floor was private.

His arm around her, giving much needed support, they crossed the foyer and went into the penthouse.

Once again it seemed to be deserted.

"We'll get a bit of sun before we change, shall we?" Thorn's question appeared to be a rhetorical one because, without waiting for an answer, he slid aside the panels and led the way onto the terrace. Lisa was in such a state of confusion that if he'd suggested abseiling down the building she'd probably have followed him without question.

The blue sky was cloudless and already the sun was warming the smooth slabs of stone beneath their feet, but she scarcely noticed.

Having helped her off with her loose jacket, he discarded his robe, and in a moment they were stretched side by side on the loungers.

It seemed an age before the blood stopped pounding in her ears, the iron bands round her chest loosened, and from being blind and deaf and stupefied her senses began to return to normal.

She blinked at the sun ricocheting from a glass sky-scraper on the horizon of her field of vision, and heard the faint, muffled roar of the traffic far below. Yet still her brain seemed dazed and sluggish, unable to take in and believe what had occurred.

Rolling his head sideways to look at her, Thorn remarked, "You've only said one word in the last ten minutes. I thought my proposal might come as a surprise, but I hardly expected it to render you speechless."

"My proposal"... So he *had* said "I want to marry you"...

After swallowing hard she managed, "You were joking, of course. Just pulling my leg."

She didn't need his silence to convince her that she was mistaken.

"*Why* do you want to marry me?" She sounded as bewildered as she felt.

"I'm after your money," he told her.

"I wish you'd be serious," she said crossly.

"You're quite right, my sweet; marriage is a serious business. In the past I've always shied away from it."

"Then you've never…?"

"Asked any other woman to marry me? The answer to that is no. I was on the verge of it once, then better sense prevailed."

"So why *me*?"

"Why do you think?"

"I've no idea," she admitted.

He smiled mockingly. "Perhaps I was waiting for Miss Right and you fit the bill."

"I don't see how I can," she said almost pleadingly. "I'm not clever or sophisticated or beautiful. I don't belong in your kind of world."

"Is my world so very different from yours?"

"I'm sure it *has* to be."

"That's guesswork on your part, mere presumption. You haven't had a chance to find out whether it is or not."

"But I'd never fit into your circle. I'm not wealthy, or socially acceptable."

"You will be when you're my wife." He sounded so sure, so *confident*. "And now we've got that settled…"

Lisa shook her head helplessly. "I don't understand *why* you want to marry a woman you've known for less than forty-eight hours."

"You must have been aware of the instant attraction, the powerful chemistry between us from the word go? It's a necessary ingredient of any good marriage."

"Yes," she admitted. "But there has to be *more* than that. Chemistry alone is merely the basis for an affair."

"You said you had no intention of having an affair with me."

"And you said you didn't want one," she shot back.

"That's true. I don't want an affair. I want to make you my wife."

She stuck to her guns. "That's what I don't understand." Wryly she added, "It's not as if I'm anything out of the ordinary. So *why*?"

When, because of the way things had worked out, he'd decided to spring his proposal on her, he hadn't imagined she'd be so difficult, so hard to persuade.

Without flattering himself he knew that because of his wealth, the kind of lifestyle he could give them most women would have jumped at the chance of becoming Mrs Thornton Landers, without ever questioning his motives for asking them. Now here was this chit of a girl spiritedly demanding to know why.

Quitting his own lounger with one smooth movement full of masculine grace, he came to sit by her side and let his eyes travel slowly from her curly head down to her slender feet and back again.

Blushing furiously, Lisa felt as if those eyes were stripping her, leaving her naked and exposed.

His leisurely appraisal of her pale gold body with its youthful curves and flawless skin completed, he bent his dark head to brush her mouth with his own.

Her instinct for self-defence fighting a rearguard action, she somehow kept her lips pressed together.

His mouth wandered away, and with his tongue-tip he explored the dimple in her chin before moving to kiss and nip at the soft skin beneath the pure line of her jaw.

It was so erotic that, unable to cope, she tried to push him away. As her palms met his sun-warmed chest he whispered, "Mmm...that's right, touch me."

She wanted to. Oh, how she wanted to! But some shred of common sense warned that once she did she'd be committed, swept away. With a great effort she kept her hands quite still.

"Open your mouth for me, Lisa," he whispered.

When she shook her head he began to suck and nibble at her lips. Unable to help herself, she gasped. Taking immediate and ruthless advantage, he covered her mouth with his own and deepened the kiss, exploring with a tongue that stroked and coaxed and darted with sensual pleasure.

She was a quivering mass of sensations when he finally lifted his head and said deliberately, "That's chemistry in action—one *very* good reason, I'm sure you'll agree. But there are more, if you want me to enumerate them?"

When she stayed mute, unable to speak to save her soul, he went on, "You're kind and sweet-natured, yet your occasional sharpness is stimulating. I like your enthusiasm, and the eager, unspoilt way you enjoy life... Though you haven't had many breaks you're happy, and you seem to carry happiness with you. That's a very rare gift.

"In a nutshell, you pleasure and entertain me in a way no other woman has. And added to that..." he smiled at her, his green eyes tender "...guess what?"

"You can't possibly love me..." She was unaware of the bright thread of hope in her voice. "You've only known me a day..."

He sighed. "And here was I thinking you had a poetic soul. Don't you know your Marlowe? 'Who ever loved that loved not at first sight?'"

Then he *did* love her. The wonderful thing that had happened to her had happened to him too. She didn't know how it could have done, but miraculously it *had*. Suddenly she was floating on cloud nine. When he smiled at her she smiled back, her face radiant.

"So are you ready to quit stalling and give me your answer?"

CHAPTER FOUR

WHILE Lisa's heart cried, Yes, oh, yes! her brain insisted that it was too soon to commit herself. She might *love* him but she didn't *know* him.

Cloud nine rocked a little.

Because of her parents' divorce and the unhappiness it had caused, she'd always been determined that, no matter how tempted, she would never rush into a relationship as serious as marriage.

Slowly she said, "I can't give you an answer just like that."

Seeing the confusion in her hazel eyes, he admitted with a sigh, "I hadn't meant to spring it on you quite so suddenly. My intention was to give you a chance to get to know me first..." With a wry little twist to his lips, he added, "But having taken the plunge, so to speak, now I'm eager to have things settled."

She shook her head. "I need time to think."

Stifling his impatience, knowing that there was no point in scaring her off altogether, he said flatly, "Very well, I'll give you a week."

Relieved not to be pressured, to have a breathing space, Lisa smiled, and he thought, not for the first time, that her smile was quite enchanting.

His expression lightening, he suggested, "Now, what do you say we get dressed and continue our sightseeing?"

Taking her hands, he rose to his feet, pulling her with him. "Tell you what," he said as they left the warmth of the terrace for the coolness of the living-room, "we'll start with a real treat. I'll buy you breakfast at McDonald's."

"Gee, thanks."

He slapped her retreating backside. "Now don't get sassy."

The glorious weather held, and over the next few days life became more hectic and exciting than Lisa could ever have envisaged. Thorn scarcely left her side, and they went everywhere and did everything, spending hours exploring the many-faceted jewel that was New York.

When she expressed concern about him being absent from the office he brushed it aside, saying, "I haven't had a real break for two years... And if the boss can't play hookey when he wants to, who can?"

Often they returned to the penthouse in the early hours of the morning, after dining and dancing the night away.

Thorn was an excellent dancer, with an almost feline grace, and Lisa fitted into his arms as if she'd been made for them. Though she'd had little experience on the dance floor, a lightness of foot and a natural sense of rhythm enabled her to follow him easily.

Every evening he bought her flowers, or candy, or—careful not to hurt her pride—some charming little memento that was too cheap for her to take exception to. He had, she soon realised, set out to court her, to win her heart. Without knowing that it was already his, she thought wryly.

From the age of sixteen she'd resisted would-be boyfriends with hands like flypaper and little finesse. A frank admission that she disliked being pawed had usually meant that she hadn't got asked out a second time. But, having no desire to lose her virginity to some callow, fumbling, sweaty-palmed youth, she'd been content to wait for the right man.

Only Ian had come anywhere near to being her ideal.

Even then she'd been able to resist his more practised attempts at seduction, not by obeying a particularly strict code of morals, but simply because, she now realised, she'd never been seriously tempted.

With Thorn, however, she was vulnerable. He only had to smile at her, touch her hand or look at her with those clear green eyes to turn her legs to water and make her go limp with longing. He was irresistible, and as the days passed her feelings grew until she was fathoms deep in love with him.

Each night when he escorted her to her bedroom door she half hoped that he'd sweep her off her feet and make love to her until all her doubts vanished. Instead he would kiss her until she was dazed and breathless, then, with a casual, "Goodnight; see you in the morning," walk away.

One night, when his mouth and his roving hands engendered an aching hunger he refused to satisfy, forgetting everything but the *need* he'd aroused, she clung to him, pressing her body against his.

Gently but firmly unwinding her arms from around his neck, he said, "Goodnight, Lisa; sleep well." Then, with undisguised mockery, he went on, "If you find you can't sleep there are plenty of books in the study."

Damn him! Oh, damn him! she thought as she stumbled into her bedroom. He knew *exactly* what he was doing to her, and he was doing it deliberately.

But it was her own fault. Instead of allowing herself to be beguiled into that state of heated excitement, she should keep him at bay.

Fat chance! She had as much hope of resisting his potent sexuality as a candle had of withstanding a blowlamp playing on it.

Making a determined effort not to think about him, to empty her mind, she climbed wearily into bed. But sleep refused to come, and after tossing and turning for a while she decided to follow his mocking suggestion.

Pulling on her thin dressing-gown, Lisa padded through the semi-darkness to the study, and, feeling for the wall switch, flooded the book-lined room with light.

There were several comfortable-looking chairs and a large, handsome desk with a fax machine and a computer. On one end of the desktop a discarded briefcase nudged an untidy pile of papers and folders, a personal diary and a spare key, proving that Thorn's dislike of clutter was easy-going rather than obsessive.

His books were an eclectic mix, Lisa discovered. Travel, biographies, hobbies, architecture, languages, the classics and the best of modern literature jostled for space on the shelves.

She had selected one of her childhood favourites—a delightfully illustrated copy of Washington Irving's *The Legend of Sleepy Hollow*—and was making her way past the desk when she brushed against the pile of papers. They overbalanced and hit the floor with a dull thud.

Muttering imprecations at her own clumsiness, she put the book down and crouched to collect the scattered documents. She was picking up a large envelope when a sheaf of photographs slid out. They were close-ups of a woman's head and shoulders.

Lisa was shovelling them back in when all at once she froze into immobility. Though she was looking at them upside down there was little doubt that the woman was herself.

With trembling fingers she turned them the right way up and stared at them. She had no knowledge of having been photographed, so whoever had taken them must have used a zoom lens. But *when* had they been taken? And *why*?

She was wearing a grey and white spotted blouse—a

garment she hadn't worn since arriving in the States—so
they had definitely been taken before she'd left England.

Yes, though the background was out of focus the building behind her was Houghton Post Office, so she must have
been walking down the main street of that quiet country
town.

So that left *why*. And the even more vexed question of
what Thorn was doing with them.

She was still staring down at the collection like someone
in a trance when his cool voice queried, "Something
wrong?"

Shock made her gasp audibly. Dropping the photographs,
she jumped to her feet, her heart clamouring, her palms
clammy. She felt both flustered and guilty, like a child
caught in some misdemeanour.

Barefoot and bare-legged, wearing only a short, maroon-
coloured robe, Thorn seemed to fill the doorway. His green
eyes were heavy-lidded and his black hair was rumpled.

As he came towards her, looking big and menacing, she
had to fight against a cowardly impulse to back away.
Standing her ground, she somehow found her voice. "I—
I came in to borrow a book...and I accidentally knocked
some papers and things off your desk."

His eyes fell on the photographs, and for a split second
he looked furious. Then, the anger swiftly masked, he said
a shade grimly, "I see...that must have been the noise I
heard... Well, if you've got your book, leave the rest of
the things where they are and I'll pick them up tomorrow."

Before she could lasso her scattered wits he had closed
the study door behind them and was shepherding her back
to her room, his hand at her waist burning through the thin
fabric of her nightclothes.

When they reached her door she gritted her teeth and
turned to face him. "Those photographs...I'd like an explanation—"

"I'll give you one tomorrow morning."

"But I—"

"It's the middle of the night," he pointed out a shade curtly. "And I for one would like to get some sleep."

With that she was forced to be satisfied, though a sneaking suspicion suggested that he was playing for time.

The book failed to hold her attention, and after a minute or two she put it aside and tried to sleep. But questions came thick and fast, battering against her tired brain like balls at a coconut shy.

Who had taken the photographs? Why had they been taken without her knowledge? What was Thorn doing with them? And when she'd asked him how he'd managed to pick her out at the airport so easily why had he lied…?

Dawn was poking intrusive fingers through the slats of the blind before her mind grew quiet and she finally slept.

The sound of determined rapping on her door awoke her. A bleary-eyed glance at her watch showed that it was almost nine o'clock.

She had just pushed herself up on one elbow when the door opened and Thorn walked in carrying a glass of orange juice. He'd never come into her room before and Lisa was thrown into a state of abject confusion.

Casually dressed in stone-coloured trousers and a dark green shirt, he looked clear-eyed and alert and dangerously attractive. While she struggled into a sitting position he crossed to the window and opened the blinds, letting in bright sunlight. Then, having put the glass on the bedside table, he sat down on the edge of the bed and surveyed her intently.

He was so close that she could smell the freshness of his aftershave, and she saw that his well-brushed black hair, still damp from the shower, was trying to curl a little.

Unwashed and dishevelled, feeling at a distinct disadvantage, she blushed.

Leaning towards her, he kissed the tip of her nose and the corner of her mouth before nuzzling his face against her throat and laving the warm hollow with his tongue.

Almost deafened by the beating of her own heart, Lisa sat absolutely still.

Drawing back, he commented, "There aren't many women who look as dewy as a rose and taste as sweet as nectar when they first wake."

Feeling that there was something phoney about the fulsome compliment, she took a steadying breath and said crisply, "Well, I'm sure you're in a position to judge."

"Cat!" But Thorn was smiling, his teeth very white against his tanned face. "Now drink your juice while I apologise for last night. I'm sorry I was short with you, but three-thirty in the morning isn't a good time for explanations." When she simply waited he asked, "So what exactly do you want to know?"

"Who took those photographs? Why were they taken? And how did they come to be on your desk?"

He answered the last question first. "Your brother gave them to me."

"Then why didn't you say so when we were driving back from the airport and I asked how you'd been able to pick me out so easily?"

Shrugging, he said, "Seeing that they'd been taken without your knowledge, I thought it best not to mention them."

She was about to jump in when he forestalled her. "Which brings me to who took them and why... Mark hadn't seen you since you were a toddler. Any woman could have turned up here claiming to be you..."

As she started to shake her head he went on, "In the kind of circles I'm talking about, stealing a passport or getting a false one made is relatively easy."

"I don't see why anyone should pretend to be me," she objected.

"My sweet innocent—" his Southern drawl was very evident "—there are rich pickings to be made."

So that was why he'd questioned her the first night, why it had seemed almost like an iterrogation...

But he was going on, "Because your father left you nothing in his will, Mark, who is a relatively wealthy man, was intending to give you a lump sum as well as providing a home and a job..."

"Oh..." she whispered.

"With that in mind, a detective agency was employed to check you out. When they were satisfied that you were who you said you were, those photographs were taken and sent over as a means of identification. Satisfied?"

Was she? The explanation was certainly slick enough. But then it *ought* to be, she decided cynically; he'd had plenty of time to think it out. And what other explanation could there be?

When she nodded he smiled and rose to his feet. "Then as soon as you're ready we'll make a start. Today I'm planning to take you across on the ferry to the Statue of Liberty..."

Thorn was a stimulating and outgoing companion, and during the long hours spent in his company Lisa had discovered quite a lot about the man beneath the macho image.

He was arrogant, certainly, yet it was an arrogance that sprang from strength rather than weakness. He held strong opinions without being opinionated, was decisive without being dictatorial, and though far from sentimental he was unexpectedly kind and caring.

This was underlined when, emerging from her room one morning, Lisa bumped into Mrs Kirk. That good lady, dressed in a tracksuit even more striking than usual, was on her way out.

"I'm away to the mission," she informed Lisa cheerfully. "Today's cleaning day and I need an early start."

"You do an awful lot there," Lisa remarked.

"I pop down for a wee while most days," Mrs Kirk agreed.

"Doesn't Mr Landers mind?" Lisa asked curiously.

"Bless you, no. It's his money that's made it all possible. If it wasn't for his support the place would have to close."

Lisa was surprised; somehow she had never thought of Thorn as a philanthropist.

Seeing that surprise, Mrs Kirk boasted proudly, "He's a fine man and no' mean. As well as the mission he funds a hospice for the sick and dying, and an animal sanctuary..."

So he certainly wasn't mean.

When, some time later, Lisa referred to what the housekeeper had told her, Thorn looked far from gratified. "Mrs Kirk doesn't usually talk too much."

"I'm glad I know," Lisa insisted. "I think it's wonderful of you."

"Well, don't put me down as some kind of saint," he said drily. "I can afford it."

Nor was he a snob.

Though Lisa's wardrobe was both sparse and simple, without turning a hair he took her to places where the women looked a million dollars.

They were lunching at Sky Windows, with its stunning view—from the hundred and seventh floor—of the Jersey coastline, when they met Carole once more.

Her beautiful face clouded with discontent, a large fair young man at her heels, she stopped by their table. Looking at Lisa with angry, resentful eyes, and at Thorn with adoring ones, she exclaimed, "Thorn, darling...!" The peevish expression disappearing as if by magic, she smiled at him brilliantly. "Did you get my invitation?"

His face guarded, Thorn rose to his feet. "I did indeed." Turning to Lisa, he said casually, "Now I must repair an omission. Lisa, this is Carole."

Lisa smiled. "How do you do?"

Looking both sulky and jealous, Carole muttered, "Hi."

"Won't you introduce us to your friend?" Thorn suggested smoothly.

When she'd complied, albeit ungraciously, the blond giant, whose name was Paul, shook hands with them both. He had a fresh, friendly face and a grip like Tarzan's. Lisa noticed that he seemed unperturbed by Carole's behaviour.

Ignoring the other two and getting back to what *mattered*, the girl asked Thorn eagerly, "And you will come to my party?"

"If the invitation includes a guest. You see, I'd like to bring Lisa."

Carole's small white teeth gnawed at her lower lip as dismay and disappointment chased across her face. After a moment she said, with a sigh of resignation and a distinct lack of enthusiasm, "Of course. Please do."

Obviously a handful of crumbs was better than no bread, Lisa thought as Paul said, "C'mon, then, honey," and, with a parting salute, led Carole away.

Once again Lisa felt heartily sorry for the girl, madly in love with a man who didn't care a fig for her or any woman.

But that wasn't true, she had to remind herself. Thorn had said he loved *her*, had asked her to marry him. Still she scarcely believed it. His sudden proposal had taken on a dream-like quality, a sense of unreality that she was unable to shake off.

As the days whirled past Lisa's first impression of Thorn as a charismatic man with a powerful sex appeal did not diminish; rather, it was added to. But as well as being bowled over by his physical attributes she developed a healthy respect for his intellect.

He had a brain as sharp as a samurai sword and, with a keen insight into character, a sure instinct for other people's strengths and weaknesses. No doubt that was what had helped to make him the top businessman he was.

As far as she herself was concerned he was intuitive, trigger-quick to divine what she was thinking and feeling. They seemed to be on the same wavelength, and although his intellect far outstripped hers they as often as not came up with the same ideas, arrived at the same conclusions, and laughed at the same things.

But though they communicated there was a side to his character that he kept locked away, and Lisa felt oddly certain that all she knew about him was what he wanted her to know.

And still puzzling her was his reaction to any mention of Mark. If she asked questions about her brother Thorn would answer as briefly as possible then change the subject, and she couldn't help but wonder what it was between the two men that put such a cold, shuttered look on his face.

That they were business rivals was the only explanation that made any sense, yet she would hardly have thought that Mark was big enough to constitute a rival. And, if there was cut-throat rivalry, surely he wouldn't have sold out to Landers Holdings?

Reluctant to ask Thorn, far from certain that he'd tell her, Lisa decided to wait until her brother returned from his trip and ask *him*.

She was still keen to see where Mark lived but, though she'd broached the subject several times, it was Friday before Thorn kept his promise to show her. Even then it was only a quick drive past the entrance to the pleasant apartment building on East Sixty-third Street.

Recalling that in his last letter Mark had mentioned that CMH Electronics had their offices only a block or so away, she asked Thorn to point them out. Reluctantly, it seemed to her, he did so.

That night he took her to the Rainbow Room for cocktails, followed by a leisurely meal. Seeing how handsome and distinguished he looked in his dinner jacket and black bow-tie, for the first time Lisa wished that instead of the simple white halter-necked dress she always wore she had something really stunning.

"What's troubling you?" he asked, as though she'd faxed her dissatisfaction.

With no time to dissemble she spoke the truth. "I was just wishing I had something nicer to wear."

He gave her hand a quick, reassuring squeeze. "You look sweet and charming. There isn't a man in the room who won't envy me."

From their luxurious eyrie on the sixty-fifth floor of the Rockefeller Center the prospect was wonderful. Manhattan stretched before them, spiky and alluring, a jagged phalanx of skyscrapers, each vying to be the tallest or the most important.

The evening sky had grown velvety dark and myriad lights were sparkling like rhinestones when, putting down her coffee-cup, Lisa remarked, "I find this kind of view absolutely breathtaking. Though I never really expected to I love being up high, the feeling of looking down on the world."

Thorn smiled a little. "So do I. That's why I chose the penthouse. Perhaps it springs from being a small-town boy."

A moment before he had waved for the bill, and Lisa

waited until it was settled and the waiter had moved away before asking, "Then you're not a native New Yorker?"

"No. I hail from Georgia…"

So that accounted for his faint and fascinating Southern drawl, she realised.

"Though my father's business interests were based in Atlanta my mother didn't care to live there, so I was brought up in Peachtree, about twenty miles to the south.

"I only settled in New York when I came back from England. But now I can't imagine living anywhere else. Despite all its faults, it's such a colourful, exciting city. Eventually it gets a hold on you."

"I can believe that," Lisa remarked. "It already has a hold on me."

"Then you'll be happy to live here?" Deliberately he added, "As my wife?"

Her heart skidded to a halt, then started to race.

The temporary reprieve was over, and she was no nearer to a decision.

She *wanted* to marry him, but quite apart from her practical doubts there was a vague feeling of disquiet, a kind of premonition that something was wrong.

Unconsciously playing for time, she said, "Marriage is such a big step…"

He remained silent, his hard-boned face wiped clear of all expression so that it was impossible to tell what he was thinking.

Flustered, her words giving away a great deal more than she realised, she suggested in a low voice, "Suppose…instead of marriage…suppose I agree to sleep with you?"

His jaw tightened and his eyes grew as cold as a glacial lake. "You told me you weren't prepared to have an affair."

"I've changed my mind."

"Well, I haven't changed mine. I said I wanted to marry you, and that still stands. It's marriage or nothing."

Green eyes trapping hers and holding them, he said adamantly, "I've given you enough time to make up your mind, and I don't intend to wait any longer. I want an answer, Lisa, and I want it now. I won't ask again."

It was an ultimatum, pure and simple.

Somehow she dragged her gaze away and, turning her head, she stared across the handsome room, with its art deco furniture and its complement of rich and famous people.

Waiters moved swiftly and silently between the tables, coffee and French perfume drifted on the air, and popping corks mingled with a subdued hum of conversation and laughter.

Her thoughts fully occupied, Lisa took in none of it.

Why was she so afraid? What was there to be afraid of? That she still didn't really *know* him? That it wouldn't work because they came from different worlds? But who could guarantee that *any* marriage would work? Life itself was a gamble.

Pushing aside her doubts and fears, she grasped at the one thing she was certain of—she didn't want to live without him. She wanted to seize life and love with both hands, to soar to the heights, and if, like Icarus, she fell to the ground it had to be better than never having flown at all...

Leaning over, Thorn took her chin in his hand and swivelled her face towards him, his fingers warm and strong against her jaw.

"Well, Lisa?" The green eyes with their mysterious pinpoints of gold held hers.

Taking a deep breath, she said steadily, "Yes, I'll marry you."

Some powerful emotion flared in his eyes. Before she

could decipher what it was it was gone, replaced by a quieter, more controlled satisfaction.

Releasing her chin, he took her left hand and, raising it to his lips, kissed the inside of her wrist, his tongue-tip finding the fluttering pulse.

Then, feeling in his pocket, he produced a small white suede box and flicked open the lid with his thumbnail. A moment later he was sliding a ring onto her third finger. It fitted perfectly.

Like someone in a dream she found herself staring down at a half-hoop of diamonds, delicate and flawless, exactly right for her slim but strong hand.

Watching her face, he said, "If you don't like it I'll make arrangements to change it."

"Oh, I do," she breathed. "It's absolutely *beautiful...*"

"But?"

Thrown by his ability to walk in and out of her mind, she stammered, "I—I just thought it must have cost an awful lot."

His white teeth flashed in a smile. "Don't worry; it hasn't broken the bank."

"Even so, I can't help but feel I'll need a bodyguard when I wear it."

Sounding unconcerned, he told her, "It's insured."

"I'm glad about that," she assured him fervently.

His glance had strayed to a spot behind her and, his expression suddenly wary, he said, "Let's get out of here."

As they rose to go a balding man with a florid complexion and a paunch hurried over and stuck out his hand. "Mr Landers... I've been hoping to see you, but your office told me you weren't available."

Thorn shook hands with the man perfunctorily as he went on, "I was in contact with your brother-in-law a week or so ago and I—"

Lisa felt Thorn stiffen. "If you'll excuse me..." his

voice icily polite, his face a frozen mask, he cut through the other man's words "...we were just leaving."

His arm around Lisa's waist, he swept her away. "Sorry about that," he said as they took the lift down. "I make it a rule never to talk business when I'm out."

To Lisa it had seemed to be more than just a decision not to talk business. There had been a strange *urgency* about Thorn's desire to get away, a brusqueness amounting to rudeness that had left a bad taste.

Perhaps he realised, because in the taxi he curved his hand round the warmth of her nape and moved his thumb in a soft, seductive caress that effectively blotted the little scene from her mind.

When they reached the penthouse he suggested, "Shall we have a drink on the terrace?" Without waiting for an answer, he slid aside the glass panels, letting in the balmy night air, and went on, "Champagne, I think, as this is a celebration."

While he found long-stemmed flutes and took a well-chilled bottle of Dom Pérignon from the fridge, Lisa made her way into the garden and sat on the canopied swing-seat.

The sharp excitement of a few minutes ago returning, she wondered if he intended to make love to her now that she was wearing his ring. When he appeared, however, and handed her a glass of champagne, his manner was brisk, more businesslike than lover-like.

Sitting down beside her, he said without preamble, "I'd like us to be married as soon as possible. The necessary formalities will have to be completed and you'll need to shop for clothes, so suppose we say in three days' time?"

In the act of sipping her champagne, Lisa choked. "Three days?" She'd been expecting much longer than that. "But why so soon?"

Green eyes gleaming, he asked, "Why do you think?"

Heat suffusing her cheeks, she began, "I still don't—"

"Neither of us has got any ties," he interrupted firmly, "so I see no reason for waiting. In fact I'm not sure how long I *can* wait and, just to confound the critics, I'd rather like a virgin bride. Virginity is a rare commodity in this day and age," he added cynically. Then, almost as an afterthought, he asked, "You are a virgin, aren't you?"

Blushing harder than ever, she nodded.

"Then if *you* want to be a virgin bride you'd better make it soon. I'm not noted for my patience..."

Already she knew him too well to believe that. He had iron self-control and could be as patient as any hunter stalking his prey... Suddenly she shivered. What had put that unfortunate simile into her mind?

Trying to ignore a chill feeling that robbed the night of its warmth, she said steadily, "I'd like to wait until Mark's home. He's all the family I've got."

"This is an open-ended trip. He might not be back for weeks," Thorn objected.

"But surely you could *get* him back?"

"Our business isn't confined to Hong Kong, and a lot of it's extempore, seizing opportunities. He's bound to be moving about a great deal..."

Lisa stuck her toes in. The two men would soon be brothers-in-law and whatever differences were responsible for Thorn's cool attitude would need to be resolved. Her soft mouth firming, she insisted, "I don't want to get married until Mark can be there."

Seeing the stubborn set to her chin, Thorn said shortly, "Very well, I'll do my best."

"Thank you." She smiled her relief.

"Then you'll marry me in three days' time?"

Her heart starting to pound as though she'd run a mile, Lisa swallowed on a suddenly dry throat, and whispered, "Yes."

As she framed the word a shiver ran down her spine. All of a flutter, she hardly knew whether it had been caused by a breath of cool night breeze feathering across her skin or a chill of unease at having committed herself.

CHAPTER FIVE

BY HER side Thorn relaxed, and Lisa distinctly heard his sigh of relief.

With an elegant economy of movement he disposed of both glasses and, shifting his position, pressed her back so that she was half lying along the swing-seat, her head on the cushioned arm.

She looked up into his dark face, which was too strong really to be termed handsome but gave an impression of extraordinary male beauty—an impression which owed a lot to the shape of his eyes and his striking bone structure.

Bending over her, his expression intent, Thorn covered her mouth with his own. Within seconds the warmth of his kiss had banished the chill—whatever its cause—and a heated excitement was taking its place.

He made love to her until she was lost to everything but the taste of his mouth ravaging hers, the feel of his hands exploring her body, and the heady, masculine scent of his skin.

Though she was swamped by her own feelings and needs, she dimly recognised and was surprised by his hunger—a hunger he seemed to be having difficulty keeping in check.

He'd *said* he was too eager to wait long, but somehow she'd scarcely believed him. Now, it seemed, he was supplying proof.

When finally he raised his dark head he looked almost as dazed by passion as she was. His long fingers brushing a wisp of silky hair away from her flushed cheek, he said thickly, ''Time to call a halt, I think, while I still can.''

Perhaps if she'd followed her instinct to put her arms round his neck and draw his mouth back to hers he might have changed his mind. But as she hesitated, unsure of herself, he took both her hands and pulled her to her feet.

She staggered a little, like someone drunk, as, an arm round her waist, he accompanied her to her bedroom door. Heart thumping, she opened it, but though he must have known that she was on fire for him he made no move to follow her inside.

In the doorway she turned, almost prepared to plead, and looked into his face. It was rigid with control, his mouth a straight line, his brows black bars above eyes still clouded with passion.

''Thorn?'' she whispered.

Shaking his head, with a crooked smile, he said, ''Good-night, Lisa,'' and walked away.

It seemed he really *did* want a virgin bride.

The following morning, as they went up in the lift after their swim, Lisa reminded him of his promise to contact Mark.

Frowning a little, Thorn said shortly, ''I intend to start for my office as soon as I've showered and changed.''

Some fifteen minutes later, looking immaculate in a pearl-grey lightweight business suit, he followed Lisa into the kitchen. Even in such smooth, civilised garb he had an indefinable air of command, a combination of personality and power that made him look tough and formidable.

Mrs Kirk was nowhere to be seen. Waving aside Lisa's offer of toast, he swallowed a cup of coffee standing by the breakfast-bar and told her, ''We've a busy day ahead, so I'll be back to collect you as soon as possible... And don't forget to put your ring on. I like to see you wearing it.'' Then, after dropping a light kiss on her lips, he was gone.

After more than a week of the closest companionship it seemed strange and lonely to be eating a solitary breakfast, and though Lisa called herself all kinds of a fool she found herself missing him.

She was sitting in the lounge, leafing through one of the daily papers, when he returned. She looked at him gladly, hopefully.

In a voice devoid of emotion he said, ''No success as far as Mark's concerned, I'm afraid, but my secretary will keep trying to locate him; she'll fax us the details if and when she manages it. About ready to start? You'll probably need a coat...''

He was right. The weather had changed dramatically and the day was cool and overcast with the threat of rain to come. New York was in a sullen frame of mind, in no mood to smile, but still Lisa loved it.

As soon as the necessary wedding formalities had been got under way, Thorn took her to one of the city's most exclusive stores. In the bridal department, entranced by the beautiful displays, Lisa smiled at him, her eyes bright with excitement.

His face fleetingly shadowed by an expression that could have been compunction at rushing her, Thorn asked, ''Would you like a conventional wedding dress?''

Lisa shook her head and, not without some faint regret for her childhood dream of floating down the aisle in a cloud of white tulle, decided, ''In the circumstances a suit would be much more practical.''

After she'd settled on an ivory silk two-piece that Thorn said looked quite charming, he insisted on buying her a trousseau ranging from gossamer-fine undies and nightwear to haute couture gowns.

She soon discovered that he displayed none of the usual

male uninterest or disinclination to shop. He had endless patience, excellent taste, and very definite ideas on how he wanted her too look. He liked simple, elegant lines and a subtle blend of colours. To some things he gave an immediate thumbs down, to others a nod of approval.

Unaccustomed to such lavish spending, Lisa was soon hot and bothered, but when she tried to protest he pointed out that as his wife she would *need* to be well dressed, adding humorously, "As far as I'm concerned you'd look beautiful wearing a bargain-basement sack, but my reputation as a good husband will no doubt depend on you doing nothing of the kind."

Recognising the truth of that, she accepted, although not without some qualms, what to most society women would have been a meagre number of clothes but to her was an extensive wardrobe.

When shoes, sandals and accessories had been added to the list he ordered all the packages to be sent to the penthouse, and asked, "Is there anything else you'd like?"

"Yes, please," she said promptly.

He raised a dark brow. "Furs? Jewellery?"

"A cup of tea."

"I could run to a pot."

"Even better."

When they got home that evening all the beautifully wrapped boxes and parcels were waiting, and so was Mrs Kirk.

Though she was forced to subscribe to the theory that, "A man's a man for a' that" it was quite obvious, she felt, that yon lassie was as innocent as a new-born bairn, and *not* the sort he should be buying clothes for!

Her grey cockscomb on end, disapprobation emanating from every pore, she advanced on Thorn. "I see you've been doing some shopping,'' she commented, her eyes sharp behind the steel-rimmed glasses.

''For a special reason,'' Thorn told her smoothly.

''And what special reason would that be?''

''Lisa needed a trousseau. We're getting married the day after tomorrow, so you can take that disapproving look off your face.''

''Married?'' the housekeeper exclaimed. Then tartly she added, ''Well, now, you've managed to find yourself a nice wee lassie instead of one of those worldly, hard-as-nails creatures; I'm glad you've had the sense to snap her up quickly.'' With an approving nod at Lisa, she stumped away.

Just for a moment Thorn looked rattled, discomfited, as though Mrs Kirk's words had hit an unexpected target.

A little surprised, Lisa was about to tease him when, saying he had a couple of phone calls to make, he excused himself and went through to his study, leaving her to unpack the various boxes.

Earlier he'd suggested that she dispose of the few clothes she'd brought with her, but some innate caution held her back, and she hung her new things alongside the old.

By the following day there was still no news of Mark, and Lisa was having to bite back her disappointment. After breakfast Thorn announced that he was going into his office for an hour or so.

''A few things have cropped up that need my personal attention, and as I'll be taking the next two weeks off to honeymoon...''

Thrilled and delighted that he was having more time off to be with her, Lisa stood on tiptoe to fling her arms round his neck and give him an impulsive kiss. It was the first time she had ever taken the initiative and kissed him.

As she drew back she saw that his dark face was set, the

skin taut over his stark cheekbones and jaw, as though her unexpected caress had upset him in some way. But a split second later the impression of a carved mask had vanished and he looked so relaxed and normal that she decided it must have been a trick of the light.

At the door he turned to enquire casually, "You weren't intending to go out?"

"I hadn't thought about it."

"It's not a very nice day and you've the rest of your life to get to know New York, so while I'm gone why don't you put your feet up and take it easy? You've been losing a lot of sleep lately..." With a glint in his eye he added, "And honeymoons can be very strenuous."

Her face growing warm, she strove to ignore his baiting and began, "If you do manage to get hold of Mark—"

"I'll tell him to drop everything and jump on the next plane."

When the door had closed behind Thorn's tall, broad-shouldered figure she found a magazine and put her feet up as he'd suggested, but she was unable to settle.

Mrs Kirk had obviously gone to the mission, and all at once, inexplicably, the luxurious penthouse began to feel like a prison.

On edge and jittery, Lisa moved restlessly, her mind a sudden jumble of disquieting thoughts. Everything had happened so quickly that her life had taken on a strange, illusory quality, and it hardly seemed real that tomorrow was going to be her wedding day. Yet it was.

She had no doubts about *wanting* to marry Thorn; still, the uneasy feeling that she'd been swept into it with undue haste persisted. If only he'd been content to wait a week or two...

Mark had been so kind, so concerned about her that she didn't want to get married without him being there or even *knowing* about it. She tried to cheer herself with the thought that if they *were* able to get hold of him this morning there was still time. But in view of their failure so far it appeared a rather forlorn hope.

If only he would contact them... Though she knew little about the world of big business it seemed odd that he should be gone so long without keeping in touch with his office.

His office...

Abruptly Lisa straightened up. It was Thorn's secretary at Landers Holdings' Madison Avenue offices who had been trying to locate Mark, but his *own* secretary at the CMH offices on East Sixty-third Street might have a better idea of his movements, might even have heard from him...

Excitement brought her to her feet. Surely it was worth a try? About to reach for the phone, she paused. It might be better to go in person. If she took a taxi she could be there in ten minutes or so, and she *needed* to get out of the penthouse for a while.

Her mind made up, she went to find a light mac and her handbag. Only when she was about to leave the apartment did it occur to her that she had no means of getting back in again.

Perhaps that was why Thorn had asked her if she planned to go out. If she'd said yes he would no doubt have given her a key.

As she stood wondering what to do, her subconscious stirred into life. Hadn't there been a spare key lying on Thorn's desk?

Ill at ease, feeling as though she had no right to be there, Lisa went into his study. This time, apart from the computer and the fax machine, the desktop was clear.

Hesitating, she bit her lip. Perhaps he'd just dropped it into a drawer? Even more uncomfortable, but reluctant to give up now, she opened the right-hand drawer, and there it was.

She had to remind herself that after tomorrow she would be mistress here before she could bring herself to reach in and take it. As she did so her eye fell on a silver-framed photograph—a studio portrait of a girl of about her own age. But there any resemblance ended.

The blonde was wearing a clinging, low-cut dress. On the vivid face there was what Mrs Kirk would no doubt have described as a *worldly* look—an overt sexiness.

Head thrown back, red lips pouting, eyes laughing straight into the camera, she looked like a young Marilyn Monroe. ''To darling Thorn, all my love, Ginny' had been scrawled across one corner in bold black writing.

Shutting the drawer with a bang, Lisa wished she'd never seen the photograph. Being reminded of Thorn's ex-lovers only served to stir up more doubts and uncertainties.

But she must forget the past, not let it bother her. *She* was the woman Thorn loved and was going to marry. Holding onto that thought, she dropped the key in her bag and hurried out of the penthouse.

Outside the heavy sky draped itself over the skyscrapers like a sagging grey blanket. A fine rain was falling, making the pavement and the sidewalks shiny, settling the summer dust. The air smelled of dampness, of gasoline and exhaust fumes.

A yellow cab was cruising by. Between the bobbing umbrellas, its eagle-eyed driver spotted her raised hand and pulled over. She called the address through his half-open window, and in a moment, feeling like a real New Yorker, was on her way.

When she had reached her destination and paid off the cab she went inside the glass and concrete office block and, having consulted the indicator board, took the lift up to the tenth floor.

The CMH offices, she discovered, were at the end of the main corridor. When she went to the reception area and

asked for Mr Hayward's office she was directed to a door
on the left. At a desk in the outer office an efficient-looking
woman with short black hair looked up to ask briskly, "Can
I help you?"

"I need to get in touch with Mr Hayward urgently and
I—"

"I'm afraid he's away on a business trip," the woman
said dismissively.

"Yes, I know, but—"

"If you can give me some idea of your business—" her
manner was brusque, impatient "—I might be able to direct
you to someone who could be of assistance."

"It's a private matter. I'm Mr Hayward's sister…" As
briefly and concisely as possible Lisa explained the situation, ending, "I'd like him to be at the wedding, so I was
hoping you might know where to contact him."

The dark eyes strayed to the hoop of diamonds on Lisa's
left hand and lingered enviously. "I'm sorry, Miss
Hayward—" the impatience was now effectively masked
"—but I have no idea of his exact location. Mrs Luten, Mr
Hayward's personal secretary, is off sick today. I'm only
on loan from the sales department."

"Oh…"

Seeing the disappointment that Lisa was unable to hide,
the woman suddenly became more human. "However, if
you'll leave it with me, I'll try and get in touch with Mrs
Luten. If she can tell me where Mr Hayward is I'll phone
or fax a message. Where can he reach you?"

"I'm staying at Mr Landers' apartment."

"Then I'll get on to it as quickly as possible."

"Thank you." Lisa smiled.

That smile lit up her face, turning her into a beauty, the
black-haired woman thought, with a sigh. All at once it was
easy to see how any man could have been bowled over.

Leaving the building in a more optimistic frame of mind,

Lisa found that the rain had stopped and the leaden sky had lightened somewhat to match her mood.

A glance along the busy street having confirmed that there were no cabs in sight, she decided to return on foot.

As she walked, automatically dodging the other pedestrians, her buoyant mood began to deflate and she became aware of a strange reluctance to go back to the apartment and face Thorn. Without knowing why, she felt instinctively that he wouldn't approve of what she'd done.

When she reached the penthouse and let herself in she breathed a sigh of relief to find it still empty. If she put the key back in the drawer he need never know she'd been out...

Oh, *really*, she thought crossly; it was ridiculous to feel so nervous, to act as though she were some kind of criminal. And all over nothing. She'd *tell* him she'd been out, *tell* him exactly what she'd done...

If she did he'd know that she'd seen that photograph, and she didn't want him to know. He might think she'd been deliberately prying.

Well, she hadn't. Her conscience was clear. But it wouldn't be if she set out to deceive him, even over such a minor thing...

She had just returned to the living-room after putting her mac away when she heard the front door open and close and his step in the hall.

Still standing, Lisa turned to him, and said with forced lightness, "You haven't been long."

"Well, I've plans for this afternoon and evening. I thought we'd go out and paint the town red—a kind of last fling before we—" Breaking off abruptly, his eyes searching her face, he demanded, "What's happened?"

"Happened?" The word emerged as a croak.

Looming over her, he gripped her upper arms and, holding her there, studied her intently. "You're all worked up over something. What is it?"

Her eyes fixed on the knot in his tie, she hesitated, wondering where to begin.

He shook her a little. "Look at me." Forced to tilt her head back, she looked into his grim face and felt a constriction in her throat. "Well, Lisa?"

Suddenly she was afraid. Her voice sounding husky and uncertain, she confessed, "I went to the CMH offices... I thought Mark's own secretary might have heard from him...might know where he was..."

Thorn's brilliant eyes narrowed into green slits and his fingers tightened painfully. "And?"

"She was away sick. When I'd explained the situation the woman I spoke to said she'd do her best to locate him— Thorn, you're *hurting* me..."

"I'm sorry." His grip loosened a little. "What else?"

"Nothing else...except that I borrowed a key from your desk drawer. I'm sorry...I hope you don't mind."

The tension seemed to drain from his big frame. "Of course I don't mind."

"Only, I remembered seeing it lying on your desktop and I—"

"There's no need to explain or apologise. I ought to have given you a key."

She drew a deep, shaky breath. "Then you're not too angry with me?"

"Why on earth should I be angry with you?"

But he *had* been angry.

Deciding to clear the air, she said, "I thought you might suspect me of prying, and—"

"That's the last thing I'd suspect you of."

"And I wasn't sure you really *wanted* Mark to get back for our wedding." At last it was out. "I wondered if perhaps there was some bad blood between you..."

"What a funny girl you are," he said half-mockingly, adding as she flushed a little, "But quite enchanting."

He dropped a kiss on her nose, then went on, "And speaking of our wedding…all the arrangements have now been finalised. We're being married at ten-thirty tomorrow morning by the Reverend Eli Jones. The ceremony will take place at the church of St Savior, and unless your brother gets home in time there'll only be a couple of witnesses present."

"Haven't you any relatives or friends who might want to come?"

His expression suddenly wintry, his voice curt, he answered, "I've no close relatives, and too many friends to make it practicable to single anyone out. Besides, the fewer people who know the better. I don't want to risk the news breaking. If the Press got hold of it they'd descend on us in droves."

"Oh…" Frowning, she realised that that was something she hadn't thought of. No wonder he'd been angry with her.

A smile softening the harsh lines of his face, he used the tip of an index finger to rub the groove that had appeared between her silky brows. "There's no need to look so worried. I don't envisage any real problems. Now, then, how about hitting the town?"

After a fun-filled afternoon at Coney Island they went to a Manhattan nightclub and danced until the early hours of the morning. Thorn held her close, his cheek against her hair, and, all her doubts banished, Lisa had never been happier.

Later, at her bedroom door, he kissed her with a passionate tenderness that seemed to melt every bone in her body, then drew back a little to study her face. She looked into his eyes and that look promised him *everything*.

Holding her face between his palms, he whispered, "To-morrow you'll be mine."

She was his now, he knew. His for the taking. But not yet. Not yet.

He was deliberately holding back, honing his appetite and hers. He could, and would, take her to paradise...

And suddenly he had the strangest conviction that, though totally different from any other woman he'd ever known, this sweet, innocent child could do the same for him.

But only when she was his wife. Only when he'd accomplished what he'd set out to do.

The following day Lisa slept late and awoke to find bright sunshine slanting into the room. While she put on jeans and a scoop-neck top—something casual until it was time to get ready for church—she thought of the old adage that went "Happy the bride the sun shines on"...

And, though some of the previous night's euphoria had vanished, she *was* happy, she told herself almost defiantly. But she'd be even happier if Mark had received her message and was able to make it home.

After a leisurely breakfast Thorn, looking darkly attractive in stone-coloured trousers and an open-necked shirt, produced a small flat case and handed it to her. When she looked at him questioningly, he said, "A wedding present."

"Oh, but I've nothing to give you."

"When we're married you'll have given me my present."

There was a strange look on his face, and instead of being thrilled by his words a feeling of unease made a shiver run through her.

Seeing that faint movement, he asked quickly, "Well, aren't you going to open yours?"

Pressing the catch with a shiny oval nail, she gave a gasp of pleasure. Lying on the black velvet was a cameo suspended from a thickly plaited silver chain.

The obverse had the profiles of a man and woman kissing, and, when she turned it over, on the reverse were clasped hands. It was an unusual and exquisite piece of work.

"Oh, Thorn..." she breathed. "I don't know how to thank you. Where did you find something so *right*?"

"I had it specially made. It's a copy of a Roman betrothal pendant. I thought you might like it."

"Oh, I do!" Her hazel eyes glowed. "It's absolutely perfect."

"Then when I've fastened it for you you can thank me with a kiss."

Though it was beautiful and romantic it seemed to hang cold and heavy, barbaric as a slave chain, around her slender throat. Shying away from that uncomfortable comparison, Lisa turned into Thorn's arms and stood on tiptoe to kiss him.

His hands cinched her waist and drew her closer, and, as his lips parted seductively beneath hers, like a lightning flash passion flared between them, setting the world ablaze, sending them both up in flames.

She was lost in everything when he reluctantly freed her mouth and, putting her away from him, said huskily, "We'd better see about getting changed or we'll be late."

By the time they were ready to leave for St Savior's there was still no sign of Mark, and Thorn confirmed that there'd been no message. He expressed a conventional but somehow unconvincing regret, and Lisa swallowed her disappointment as best she could as he escorted her down to their taxi.

The old stone church, with its dusty, ornate façade and its squat steeple, was incongruously sandwiched between two towering glass and concrete skyscrapers. Inside it was dim and solemn, lozenges of coloured light from its stained-glass windows lying along the polished back of the pews and the frayed red carpet.

Standing by the chancel steps, bareheaded, wearing her ivory silk suit and carrying a simple spray of apricot rose-buds, Lisa felt nervous and unsure.

Beside her, breathtakingly handsome in a pearl-grey summer-weight suit, a white carnation in his buttonhole, Thorn looked assured and coolly in control. Yet when it was discovered that the witnesses hadn't turned up, and there was a delay while two new ones were found, he visibly chafed, impatient as Jane Eyre's Mr Rochester.

Despite the warmth of the day the air inside the church was dank and chill. Whether it was due to that or to nerves Lisa wasn't sure, but she shivered all through the brief ceremony.

Though she made her responses in a clear voice the whole thing seemed as unreal as a play. The only thing she was sure of was her love for Thorn. It ran through her entire being, a rod of steel, with all her doubts and uncertainties fluttering round it like ribbons on a maypole.

Thorn appeared to have no doubts whatsoever.

When the wide, engraved ring, which she hadn't previously seen, had been placed on her finger and they had been declared man and wife, he lifted her hand to his lips. There was an arrogant satisfaction in the tilt of his black head, a glint of triumph in his green eyes, and any worries she might have had about his love for her should have been set at rest.

This wasn't a man going reluctantly into wedlock but a bridegroom who knew exactly what he was doing, who had got precisely what he wanted.

Having signed the legal documents with bold strokes, he thanked the Reverend Eli Jones, shook hands with the elderly couple who had agreed to be witnesses, and, an arm round Lisa's waist, hurried her out to the waiting taxi.

In a surprisingly short space of time they were back home. Once again, to Lisa's surprise, Thorn asked the driver to wait.

When they got to the penthouse Mrs Kirk was ready with hearty congratulations, a single-tier wedding cake and a bottle of chilled champagne. Horrified to discover that they hadn't had a single photograph taken, she produced a camera and insisted on them posing in traditional style as they cut the cake.

While they ate a piece and sipped the sparkling wine Thorn glanced at his watch and remarked, ''We haven't a lot of time.''

''Well, your cases are all packed and waiting,'' the housekeeper said cheerfully, ''and I've left a two-piece out for Mrs Landers to travel in.''

''Mrs Landers'... It scarcely seemed possible that she really *was* Thorn's wife. The thought was still running through Lisa's mind when the rest of the sentence penetrated. Glancing at him, she asked, ''Are we going somewhere?''

''Didn't I mention a honeymoon?'' he enquired blandly.

''You didn't say we were going away...'' Then, with a faint uneasiness that she was unable to account for, she asked, ''Where *are* we going?''

''I'm keeping our destination a surprise.'' His smiling glance teasing her, he added, ''We'll need to start for the airport as soon as you've changed.''

When Lisa had replaced her wedding outfit with a floral skirt and top and Thorn had discarded his buttonhole they were ready to go. Mrs Kirk, her usually dour face wreathed in smiles, came to the door to wave them off. Thorn shook hands with her gravely and thanked her for everything,

while Lisa gave her an impulsive hug that left her pink
with pleasure.

In a few minutes the newly-weds were back in the taxi
and heading for La Guardia. There, to Lisa's surprise,
Thorn's executive jet was awaiting them, reinforcing yet
again the extent of the wealth and power that her new husband wielded.

After a smooth take-off a steward served them with
smoked-salmon sandwiches and more champagne. Lisa
wanted to pinch herself.

"Things happening a bit too fast?" Thorn queried, seeing the dazed expression in her wide hazel eyes.

"I feel rather like Alice in Wonderland," she admitted.

"Poor baby," he mocked gently. "Never mind; when
we reach Jacob's Key you'll have plenty of time to relax
and catch up."

"Jacob's Key?"

"The word key comes from *cayo* or 'little island'. Jacob's Key is off the coast of Florida."

"Oh…"

The backs of his fingers gently stroked her cheek before
his hand moved beneath the riot of glossy brown curls to
settle on the warmth of her nape. "And Jacob's Castle is
ideal for a honeymoon," he added deeply.

It was an unusual name for a hotel, she thought, and,
trying not to sound breathless, she queried, "Then you
know it?"

"Oh, yes. It has everything we'll need—privacy, a comfortable king-sized bed, and no distractions."

Excitement prickled along her nerve-ends, her stomach
clenched, and molten heat ran through her. "What's the
island like?" Somehow she succeeded in keeping her voice
cool and level.

But he *knew* and that knowledge was implicit in his
mocking glance as he answered smoothly, conversationally,

"Quite green and picturesque. It has palm and pine trees, and some South American hardwood. On the lee side there's a man-made beach, and, beyond, salt-tolerant mangroves."

She wrinkled her smooth brow. "A *man-made* beach?"

"The keys—and there are about a hundred of them—are composed of ancient coral. Because the living coral reefs which surround them stop the sand-producing waves pounding in from the Atlantic there are very few natural beaches."

"How big is Jacob's Key?"

"Not big enough for an airstrip," he answered, reading her thoughts. "At Miami we change to a helicopter..."

The change was made with the smooth efficiency which characterised all Thorn's arrangements, and only minutes after leaving the plane they were whirling into the cloudless sky. It was the first time Lisa had travelled in what the grizzled pilot referred to as a "chopper", and she found it thrilling, if noisy.

From the shouted technical conversation between the two men she gathered that Thorn was also an experienced pilot. Proving that she was getting to know the man she'd married, she found herself unsurprised.

Looking down, to landward she could see the flat, grassy prairies and mangrove-surrounded waterways of what she guessed were the Everglades, and, offshore, countless tiny islands scattered like opals in the lapis lazuli-coloured sea.

Sailboats and powerboats and boats of all kinds were dotted about, and ahead lay the curve of the main keys from Key Largo to Key West.

"See the bridges?" Thorn leaned towards her and she could feel the firm pressure of his thigh against hers as he said in her ear, "There are forty-two on the Overseas Highway; they link most of the inhabited keys..."

Under cover of the noise, he went on, ''But who cares about such mundane things? All I've really thought about today is tonight…feeling your naked body beneath mine…hearing your sighs and moans as I make love to you in every way there is…finding out what pleases you most and teaching you what pleases me…sleeping with my face pillowed against your breast…''

To her horror Lisa could feel hot colour pouring into her face and her nipples firming beneath the silky material of her two-piece. She heard Thorn's soft, satisfied laugh and gave him a beseeching glance before turning away, scarlet-cheeked, to stare desperately out of the window.

As he began to speak again she felt the urge to cover her ears in self-defence, but he was pointing, saying, ''There's Jacob's Key, ahead and to the right. We'll be landing in a minute or so…''

CHAPTER SIX

As THEY flew over the scattering of islands, Lisa, following Thorn's pointing finger, picked out a green, elongated strip about three times as long as it was wide. They circled to land and she could see between the trees what looked like a castle of lightish grey stone complete with turrets, crenellated walls and a moat. It was built around a square court.

She'd thought Jacob's Castle an odd name for a hotel, but in this kind of setting she hadn't expected it to look like a castle.

There was no sign of life as they dropped down to land in the courtyard. When they came to rest Thorn slid open the door and jumped out. He reached out his strong right hand and helped Lisa to the ground.

Ducking beneath the whirring blades, the noise deafening, the turbulence tearing at her clothes and curls like a sirocco, she moved out of range before, feeling battered, dishevelled, like some kind of survivor, she turned to look back.

Thorn was exchanging a few shouted words with the man at the controls while he dealt with the luggage. As soon as the cases had been taken out the pilot gave a friendly salute and the silver machine lifted off again into the blue sky. Slit-eyed against the glare, they watched until it had cleared the treetops and was dwindling into the distance.

It was hot even in the shade and, unknotting his tie, Thorn pulled it free of his collar and, rolling it loosely, pushed it into his pocket before undoing the top three buttons of his shirt.

Her eyes fixed on the strong, tanned column of his throat, Lisa swallowed.

Seeing that little betraying reflex, his eyes glinted, and she looked hurriedly away, surveying the deserted courtyard. After the previous turmoil everything seemed oddly still and silent.

"You'd think we were alone on the island," she remarked lightly.

His white teeth gleamed in a smile. "We are."

"You're joking, of course…" But even as she spoke she knew that he wasn't. Despite the heat a sudden chill feathered across her skin, making her shiver. "The hotel—" she began helplessly.

"It isn't a hotel, merely a house…" He picked up their luggage and headed across the courtyard towards a large studded door with long leaded windows at each side of it and stout hurricane-shutters fastened back. "After my father bought Jacob's Island he had part of it modernised to use as a holiday home."

And now, presumably, Thorn owned the whole shebang.

"But it's so…bizarre…" she protested.

"It's certainly different," he agreed. "But Jacob Stein was an eccentric—a millionaire who wanted privacy and security. In the 1920s he bought the island and built this place—which was immediately nicknamed Jacob's Castle."

"Where on earth did he get the stone?" Despite all the more important questions seething in her mind it was the inconsequential that surfaced.

"It's coquina, or coral rock," Thorn answered as he put their cases down and fitted an ornate key into the large lock. "It was quarried close by. You'll have to watch you don't graze yourself on it. The surface is quite rough, except underfoot where it's been worn smooth.''

Throwing the door wide, he ushered her into a paved central hall that ran the width of the house and was open to the rafters.

Looking as stunned as she felt, Lisa gazed about her. At the far end was another door, flanked by windows, and on the right-hand side a dark wooden staircase ran up to a circular gallery. The hall was furnished as a dining-room, and on the refectory table stood a bowl of fresh pink and green speckled orchids.

Still trying to come to terms with the situation, her eyes on the waxy blooms, Lisa asked, "But if there really *isn't* anyone one else on the island, who takes care of things?''

"Duggan's—a service outfit in Key Largo. I let them know when I'm coming down and they clean and provision the place ready for me. It's not such a big job. I only use the rooms on the right of this modernised wing. The rest of the house has been closed up since old Jacob's time…''

He'd said "I'… Did he usually fend for himself when he came? Lisa wondered.

Apparently reading her thoughts, he added, "Duggan's also supply temporary staff if needed. But as this is our honeymoon—" his drawl was more pronounced and he gave her a glance that made her toes curl "—I rather liked the idea of us being entirely alone.''

Then, in a brisker tone, he added, "Now would you care to look around downstairs before I take the cases up?''

Like someone in a dream she followed him through a suite of panelled rooms with long windows, ornate plaster ceilings and open fireplaces filled with flowers. Each room had comfortable, up-to-date furniture, and the well-equipped kitchen could have belonged in any New York apartment.

A frown tugging her silky brows together, she said, "I

still don't understand how you manage here. Where do you get your power supply and drinking water?''

''There's a generator and a couple of large fresh-water tanks that are always kept full... Ready to see the upstairs?''

A quick glance showed that there were two pleasant bedrooms with *en suite* bathrooms, overlooking the courtyard, and, at the front, one big room with a bathroom at either side of it.

Lisa followed Thorn into the sunny master bedroom and while he disposed of their cases—hers on a blanket chest near the walk-in wardrobes, his own on a rack opposite—she crossed to the window. One of the casements had been left partly open to let in the warm, sweet air. Opening it wider, she leaned her elbows on the sill and stared out.

There was a wonderful view across the moat and subtropical vegetation to the beach, where the low evening sun sparkled on the blue water and the spindly trunks of the palms cast long black shadows over the pale sand.

She watched, smiling, as a trio of pelicans flew past in stately formation before ditching with ungainly ease to join the flotilla already bobbing on the water. In the distance she could see the flattish green bulk of another island...

Suddenly her breath caught in her throat as Thorn came silently to stand behind her. He drew her back against his hard body and slid his hands up to cup her breasts.

His mouth moved seductively up and down the side of her neck, kissing and nibbling, finding the soft skin beneath her jaw while his thumbs began to brush over her nipples. As they firmed beneath his teasing, one hand left her breast and, after deftly undoing the waistband of her buttonthrough skirt, slid inside to circle lightly over her flat stomach and stroke a sensuous path to her thighs.

No callow, fumbling boy, this. Burning through her delicate undies, that sure, experienced touch set her quivering with anticipation, promising a delight that she could still only guess at.

The stimulation continued, sending a torrent of fire coursing through her veins, making her throat go dry and her head spin until she was dizzy with wanting. But, instead of going on to satisfy the need they'd aroused, all at once the hands stilled and withdrew, and the big frame, which had been half supporting hers, began to move away.

An inarticulate murmur of disappointment rising in her throat, Lisa turned. Looking into her flushed face and fever-bright eyes, Thorn smiled a little, and the infuriating irony of that smile, mixed with a touch of equally infuriating sympathy, told her that he knew exactly what he had done to her, what he'd made her feel.

But why did he need to do that? Was it just a macho urge to prove that he could do it? To punish her…but for *what*? To make her beg? If it was, it was unkind and humiliating, hardly the behaviour of a man who loved her.

If he loved her. Though she'd tried to bury her doubts they'd refused to die. But if he *didn't* love her why had he rushed her into marriage? That same unanswerable question kept recurring. Though she loved him, in many ways he remained an enigma…

While he watched her, waiting for her reaction, she stared back into his dark face and thought, How irresistible! How sexy! That cool power, combined with the austere sensuality of his mouth and his ironic eyes, would make any woman mad for him.

But, resentful of his easy mastery, of the way he'd deliberately aroused her—and she was *damned* if she'd beg—Lisa fastened her skirt and remarked with as much insouciance as she could muster, "I suppose I ought to unpack."

Some emotion leapt briefly in his green eyes, but all he said was, "While you do I'd better check that the generator is working OK. It can be temperamental." Taking off his jacket, he tossed it over a chair, and, opening his case, changed into casual trousers, a cotton-knit shirt and sneakers.

Very conscious of his movements, but taking care not to glance in his direction, Lisa began to hang up her things, finding that Mrs Kirk had, with a fine disregard for price or fashion, packed her old clothes along with the new.

On his way out Thorn paused in the doorway and said urbanely, ''You must be hungry. When you've finished come on down to the kitchen. Duggan's staff have left a meal all ready.''

Endeavouring to hide the excitement she was still labouring under, Lisa nodded without speaking.

He hesitated, as if about to say something else, then changed his mind and went. It was a relief.

While she cooled down and her pulse rate returned to normal she finished putting away her things and stowed the case on one of the shelves in the wardrobe.

Should she unpack for Thorn? she wondered. Well, there was no one else to do it and, still feeling aggrieved, she was in no hurry to join him, so she might as well take up her wifely duties.

Sighing, she wished she knew more about men. Having been brought up in a household of women, she even found handling a man's clothes strange.

Having stowed everything away neatly in his wardrobe and chest of drawers, she reached for his discarded suit and put it on a hanger. As she did so she noticed the tie protruding from his jacket pocket. She pulled it out, and with it came a screwed-up ball of paper which rolled under the chair.

When she'd hung the tie on a rack alongside the others she stooped to pick up the ball of paper. She had tossed it onto the chest of drawers when she caught sight of her own name. Frowning, she smoothed it out and discovered it was a fax. It had arrived at nine-thirty that morning and was addressed to herself. The message it contained was brief and to the point.

Lisa, for God's sake don't marry Landers. Starting home immediately. Will explain everything as soon as I get back. Mark.

Staring down at the urgent words, she knew that all her doubts and fears had been justified. *Something* was badly wrong, otherwise why should Mark have sent such a message and Thorn have gone to such lengths to keep it from her?

A faint sound made her glance up. He was standing in the doorway, his black hair attractively rumpled, a lock falling over his forehead as though he'd run his fingers through it.

Smiling at her, he said, "I was wondering where you'd got to..." The smile died from his lips as he saw her strained face. "What's the matter?"

Wordlessly she held out the crumpled fax.

For a moment he was visibly disconcerted, then the fury and dismay were quickly hidden. Raising a mocking brow, he queried, "Exercising what women seem to regard as a wife's prerogative?"

"If you mean have I been going through your pockets, the answer is no. When I pulled your tie out this came with it."

"I was a fool to leave it there," he said ruefully.

"Why didn't you show it to me? I had a right to see it."

Sounding unrepentant, he admitted, "I didn't want you to get cold feet and upset all our plans at the last minute."

She took a moment or two to work it out, and then everything dropped into place. "I bet you never even *tried* to contact him," she accused. "You knew quite well he wouldn't approve of us marrying. No wonder you wanted to rush it through while his back was turned.''

Thorn shrugged. ''It seemed the easiest option. And do you really *care* whether he approves or not?''

''Yes, I care! He's my brother and I love him.''

''You don't even know him.''

Rattled by the dismissive words, she said, ''Any more than I really know you.''

A gleam in his eye, he came and took her in his arms. ''Well, there's one way you can get to know me better.''

But when he tried to kiss her, standing stiffly in his embrace, she turned her head away. ''I want to know what's wrong between you and Mark.''

''Ever heard of natural male rivalry?'' He spoke half-jokingly, making light of it.

''Yes...but it has to be more than that.''

''OK, so we hate each other's guts.''

''Why?''

He began to plant soft baby kisses along her half-averted jawline. ''Tonight is our wedding night; we've better things to do than talk.''

''I want to know,'' she said obstinately.

''I'll tell you everything tomorrow.''

She turned her head and looked him straight in the eye. ''Now.''

Just for a moment anger flared in his eyes. Once again it was swiftly masked. Wryly he said, ''I keep forgetting how young you are. Young and impatient...'' His voice deepened. ''But don't tell me you're not even more impatient for...other things...'' She flinched as his hand lightly encircled her throat and his thumb moved to rest against the pulse that fluttered there. ''More exciting things.''

He drew her against him, and as soon as she felt the hard heat of his body she started to shiver. The hand slipped up her throat and tilted her head back. A moment later his mouth was on hers, forcing her lips apart, deepening the kiss with a passionate concentration that made her very bones turn to water.

But while her body melted instantly part of her brain remained cool and unmoved, aware that he was deliberately using his expertise to subdue her, not as a male animal but for his own ends.

She wanted him—God knew she wanted him—but not at *any* price, not by sacrificing her pride and self-respect, her right to be treated as an equal.

When it came to the physical side of marriage a man like him would undoubtedly be the dominant partner, and that she might even like. But she wasn't going to let him use sex to subjugate her.

Making no effort to free herself, she forced her heavy lids open and used all her will-power to resist the drugging sweetness that was making her body yielding and languorous.

He knew at once.

His hands gripping the soft flesh of her upper arms, he lifted his dark head and stared down at her. Softly, dangerously, he ordered, "Stop fighting me, Lisa."

The look in his green eyes made her quail. She swallowed hard and, her voice scarcely above a whisper, managed, "I don't want to be treated as though I'm some mindless sex object—" The words ended in a gasp as his fingers tightened painfully.

With a kind of raging calm he asked, "Then how *do* you want to be treated?"

"With respect."

A flicker of something that could have been admiration came and went in those brilliant eyes.

Her face pale but her voice steady, she said, "I have a right to know what's wrong between you and Mark; why he was so set against me marrying you."

"Very well, I'll tell you." His grip relaxed and he freed her. "I suggest you sit down. It's not a pretty story."

Feeling as limp as a wet rag, Lisa was only too pleased to obey. As she dropped into the nearest chair Thorn went to the window and, his hands thrust deep into his pockets, his back to the room, stood staring out.

While she waited for him to speak, with a kind of hunger her eyes noted his mature width of shoulder and strong neck muscles, his neat ears and well-shaped skull, the way his black hair curled a little into his nape.

He remained silent for so long that she was starting to think he'd changed his mind when he began, in a flat voice utterly devoid of emotion. "I was thirteen years old and an only child when my mother died. Two years later my father married a young blonde widow with a ten-month-old daughter. The baby's name was Virginia, but everyone called her Ginny."

So the photograph had been of his *stepsister*, not an ex-girlfriend as she'd thought.

He went on, "The next couple of years weren't too comfortable. I never really liked my new stepmother, and distrusted her motives for marrying my father. That distrust turned to disgust when, on one of the nights he was away, she came into my bedroom with no clothes on. I was barely seventeen."

Lisa felt an answering wave of disgust and sympathy. That helped to explain why at times she'd sensed in him an underlying contempt for women.

"My father and I had always been close, and, wanting to leave without him asking awkward questions, I persuaded him that a year travelling round the world before I started university would do more for my education than time spent in school.

"Over the next four years I saw scarcely anything of the

family. When I was down from Oxford I used the long vacations to travel on the Continent.

"As soon as I left college Father wanted me to join him in his business, which was going through a sticky patch. But for obvious reasons I'd made up my mind not to return to Atlanta.

"With only a few weeks to go, I was wondering how best to break the news, when fate took a hand. Our family house was burnt to the ground. Both my father and step-mother died in the fire, but by some miracle seven-year-old Ginny was saved.

"I flew home immediately. As soon as everything was sorted out I took the child and moved to New York. She was having bad nightmares, so I thought it best to get right away.

"After renting a brownstone house in Greenwich Village I advertised for a housekeeper. I was lucky enough to find Mrs Kirk, who proved to be a treasure."

Pausing, he turned to face Lisa. "I expect you're wondering what all this has to do with Mark? Well, I'm coming to that, but I wanted you to understand the background."

Running a hand round the back of his neck as though to relieve the tension, Thorn went on, "Over the next ten years Ginny grew into a beautiful girl—happy and popular, full of innocent high spirits, and sexy as hell."

Bitterness in his tone, he added, "But what with concentrating on getting my father's business on its feet again, and then building my own little empire, I hardly noticed.

"Though she looked older, she was barely seventeen when, while I was away on a business trip, she eloped, not with a college boy but with an experienced man over ten years older than her. By the time I caught up with them they were married."

As realisation dawned Lisa's hazel eyes widened.

"That's right," Thorn said savagely. "Mark was my brother-in-law even before *our* wedding."

"I—I don't understand why you're so angry about it," Lisa stammered. "I know there was quite an age-gap, but at least he wasn't a fortune hunter…and presumably Ginny *wanted* to marry him."

"They'd been having an affair behind my back and she was pregnant!"

"But I still don't see why—"

Thorn cut through her words ruthlessly. "And despite the fact that she was having his baby it wasn't long before he started to ill-treat her."

"Oh, *no*…" Lisa whispered.

"When I noticed bruises on her arm one day she burst into tears and confessed that Mark knocked her about. I went to see him and told him what I'd do if it didn't stop. He swore he hadn't laid a finger on her, and advised me to mind my own damned business."

So Mark could be no weakling if he'd stood up to Thorn at his most formidable, Lisa thought.

"A few weeks later, during one of their frequent quarrels, she tumbled down a flight of stairs and lost the baby. I went to see her in hospital and she broke down and as good as admitted he'd pushed her. I told her to leave the swine and come home."

Horror-stricken, Lisa stared at Thorn's bleak face.

"When I made it clear she wasn't going back to him he accused me of interfering, and worse…"

"Worse?"

"He alleged that I was in love with her myself, that I was jealous."

With a sudden, vivid mental picture of Ginny's photograph, of the pose, which had been flaunting, anything but sisterly, Lisa asked quietly, "And were you?"

Thorn looked genuinely taken aback "Certainly not,"

he answered shortly. "I never thought of Ginny as anything but a child, a much younger sister."

Almost to himself, and in a voice full of anguish, he added, "A sister I failed... A few days later she was dead from an overdose of drugs. They were satisfied that it was an accidental overdose, but she wouldn't have been taking drugs if your precious brother hadn't driven her to it.

"My first impulse was to break his neck with my bare hands, but when the red mist cleared better sense prevailed. There had to be other ways of making him pay for the way he'd treated her."

"I don't understand," Lisa began shakily. "If there's all this bad blood between you, why did he sell out to you?"

"He didn't," Thorn said, his smile thin. "Because of CMH's recent cash-flow problems I acquired the controlling interest without his knowledge or consent. He still doesn't realise he's working for me. It's taken me the best part of a year, but now I've got him just where I want him..."

The look of savage triumph on Thorn's face was frightening as he held out his hand, palm uppermost, and slowly closed it into a fist.

Lisa shuddered. "If you hate Mark so much I don't understand why you wanted to marry his sister..."

But even as she spoke understanding came in a flash, making everything *hideously* clear. In a civilised society Thorn had been unable to exact the vengeance he wanted, so he was working on the principle of "an eye for an eye". Mark had married *his* sister...

All the blood drained from her face, blackness engulfed her, and she swayed as the room began to whirl sickeningly... A second later she felt Thorn's hand on the back of her neck, pushing her head down between her knees.

As he stood over her he cursed silently. Though she would have had to know sooner or later he had hoped to make the marriage a real one, bind her to him with ties of passion, before she realised the whole truth.

Now it would be much more difficult. She wanted him, he knew, but he also knew that she had spirit and stubbornness and pride.

After a moment or two Lisa's faintness began to pass. When she stirred and made a determined effort to sit up Thorn helped her.

Her eyes huge, dark pools in her white face, she looked at him and remembered their very first conversation, when she'd asked, "What do your enemies call you?" and he'd replied, "Ruthless."

Oh, yes, she thought bitterly, he was certainly that. Without a trace of pity he'd set out to sweep her off her feet, to make her fall in love with him and marry him.

And he'd been very thorough. To prevent any hitches to his plan he'd played the part of a gaoler, never letting her out of his sight, doing his best to see that she didn't venture out alone.

No wonder she'd sometimes felt like a prisoner... And no wonder he'd been so angry when she'd gone to Mark's office. If her brother had come back too soon the final and most important part of Thorn's plan wouldn't have worked.

And it had been a close thing. If only she'd seen Mark's fax *before* the wedding, instead of when it was too late to save her.

Later she might feel pain, but now, as though something had died inside her, all she was aware of was a feeling of coldness, a kind of hollow emptiness. Perhaps it was the shock.

Through stiff lips she said, "If you were looking for ways to make Mark pay, finding out about me must have been a bonus."

"It was indeed."

She flinched from his cruelty. Then, recovering a little, she asked numbly, "How *did* you find out?"

"I had detectives checking on him, looking for anything and everything that might come in handy."

"Then it was *your* detectives who took those photographs?"

"You catch on quick," he said admiringly. "I'd already laid my plans, but I wanted to make certain I was meeting the right woman."

"How did you manage to get rid of Mark?"

Thorn frowned. "I set up a last-minute business deal that was crucial to CMH's survival. He had no option but to go.

"Before he left he arranged for Mrs Simpson, his housekeeper, to meet your flight and take you back to his apartment. That was the tricky part. I didn't want her raising the alarm when she couldn't find you."

Knowing that he was quite unscrupulous, and wondering to what lengths he would have gone, Lisa stared at him with a sort of fearful fascination.

Sounding grimly amused, he said, "I didn't have her done away with, if that's what you're thinking."

Flushing, Lisa asked, "So what did you do?"

"Mrs Simpson and Mrs Kirk attend the same church, and as luck would have it Mrs Kirk mentioned that Mrs Simpson had been about to start her vacation the weekend you were due to arrive. She'd been intending to Greyhound it across to Minneapolis to visit her elderly parents.

"I went to see her and told her there'd been a last-second change of plan. It had been decided that *I* would meet you and you would stay at *my* apartment with Mrs Kirk to take care of you until Mark came home, which left her free to go on vacation. She was extremely grateful." With satisfaction, he added, "I put her on the bus myself before I came to meet you."

"And all you had to do then," Lisa said bitterly, "was persuade me to marry you. My being so green must have been a great help, made it all too easy."

"If you'd been a different kind of girl, attracted by wealth or position, it would have been a great deal easier."

"You mean your conscience needn't have pricked you?"

She saw by the way his jaw tightened that he didn't like that.

Pressing home her advantage, she tried another dart. "Wouldn't it be funny if you'd gone to all this trouble for nothing? Mark may not care two hoots that you've married me."

"He'll care."

Recalling the fax, she rather thought that Thorn was right. But, refusing to admit it, she persisted, "If he's the kind of heartless brute you say he is, I fail to see why he should be concerned in the slightest."

"Oh, I think he will be."

"And you're hoping to worry him?"

"I intend to make him sweat." It was said almost pleasantly. "In fact I should imagine he's already started. He's probably in a flat spin trying to find out where I've taken you. I dropped a hint to Mrs Kirk that I was considering Hawaii, and I asked my secretary to book two seats to Oahu, so it should take him a day or so to arrive here."

"You really think he'll come?"

"He'll come." It was said with quiet certainty.

"Then you'll expect me to show him my bruises?"

His lips thinning, Thorn stated curtly, "I've no intention of ill-treating you."

"Why not?" she cried recklessly. "If I'm to be sacrificed for your own ends you might as well make full use of me."

Stung, he drawled, "Oh, I intend to."

His meaning was quite clear and her blood ran cold.

Biting her lip until she was sure that her voice would be steady, she said, "I won't sleep with you."

He smiled mockingly. "I rather thought you were looking forward to it. You were eager enough to sleep with me before we were married. What's the difference now?"

All the difference in the world. Then she'd loved him and believed—or almost believed—that he loved her. Now she knew that his only intention had been to *use* her, and she hated him for the way he'd deliberately lied and deceived her.

Oh, yes, he'd take her to bed to consummate the marriage, and because she was the only woman available, but she was nothing to him except the means of wreaking his revenge.

"You're a rotten, heartless—" She choked.

Clicking his tongue, he chided, "That's no way for a wife to speak to her husband."

"But I'm *not* your wife, and I never will be."

"Oh, I think you will." He sounded unperturbed.

She shook her head. "I'm leaving."

"How?"

The monosyllable brought her up short. He'd chosen their honeymoon venue well.

Infuriated by the derisive gleam in his green eyes, she retorted, "Swim if I have to."

"The nearest island is a mile away."

"Drowning would be preferable to sleeping with you."

"Later I'll see if I can't change your mind about that."

"You'll have to use force."

Thorn smiled grimly. "I rather doubt it."

But he hadn't said he wasn't prepared to...

CHAPTER SEVEN

As SLOW shudders began to run through Lisa, Thorn held out his hand and asked casually, "Now are you coming to get something to eat?"

Struggling for composure, she was about to shake her head when she thought better of it. Though her appetite had vanished she wanted to get away from the bedroom with its tense atmosphere and that emotive bed.

Without answering, and studiously avoiding both his hand and his eyes, she got to her feet and started for the door. She had taken just one step when steely fingers closed around her wrist, bringing her to an abrupt halt.

She turned to look at him with big, scared eyes. There was an arrogant sensuality about his mouth, and his eyes held hers commandingly. "Let's get one thing clear," he said softly. "I have no intention of allowing you to sulk. So if you prefer to go straight to bed—"

"No!" Fighting down the panic, she managed, "I—I'd like something to eat."

His green eyes still pinning her, he released her wrist and held out his hand. Biting her lip, she put hers into it. Coward! Coward! she berated herself silently. But what was the point of precipitating what she feared most?

They went downstairs hand in hand like lovers. As always his touch made her tremble. But this time, she told herself, it was because she *hated* it so.

In the attractive kitchen on a covered trolley, an excellent cold meal awaited them. Thorn pulled out a chair for her, and, when she was seated, helped her to a tempting array of fresh pink seafood and some crisp green salad.

"Thank you." Her voice was cool and brittlely polite.

"Champagne?"

"No, thank you, I…" About to say she had nothing to celebrate, she changed it to "I've had enough for one day."

Her stomach churning, anything but hungry, she buttered a roll and made a pretence of eating. Becoming aware that he was watching her, a frown dragging his black brows together, she did her best to force down a little of the salad before pushing away her plate.

Impatience edging his tone, he asked, "Is that all you're going to eat? You've had scarcely anything today."

"I find I'm not really hungry." With a spark of spirit, she added sweetly, "I can't *imagine* why."

As though the shot had gone home, his dark face seemed to hollow and tauten, the hard bone structure showing starkly, but, making no comment, he reached to pour coffee for them both.

While they drank in silence Lisa watched him covertly from beneath long, curly lashes. He wore a look of introspection, as though examining his own thoughts and feelings, but, judging by the grim set to his jaw, whatever he'd found had given him no particular pleasure.

After a moment or two his expression cleared, and, his attitude as casually normal as if that shattering scene in the bedroom had never taken place, he suggested, "Shall we stretch our legs?"

The idea appealed, and she got to her feet with alacrity. Still mentally off balance, she needed time to regain some kind of equilibrium before she could think straight and start to come to terms with what had happened.

At the far end of the living-room French doors opened onto a paved terrace with a short flight of steps leading down to a wooden drawbridge that spanned the moat. Out-

side, the low evening light was as golden as honey, and the
balmy air carried the fragrance of tree-orchids and frangi-
pani and a salt tang from the sea.

Apparently intent on keeping things on a friendly footing, as they crossed the drawbridge Thorn began to tell her
about the moat.

"It's seawater, of course, but though it rises and falls
with the tide a clever system of engineering means that it
never completely empties. At the end, where the wall is
built out—" he pointed "—there's a mooring for boats..."

Lisa walked beside him, only half listening, a prey to the
fears and anticipations of what the coming night might
bring. Soon it would be time for bed and she still had no
idea what to do.

But what *could* she do? She was alone here with him. If
he was determined to make this marriage a real one, even
if she struggled his strength was so much greater than
hers... But would he really use force to have his way?

Despite his undoubted ruthlessness, she suddenly felt
certain that he wouldn't. A sure instinct told her that though
he might use all his expertise to *seduce* her he wasn't a
man who would force a woman. He would want her warm
and willing and responsive.

So her best, her *only* defence was to stay cold and unmoved. *If she could.* Though she hated him now for what
he'd done to her, her body still longed for his domination,
still craved the delight and satisfaction he could give it.

Well, her *will* would control her errant body, she vowed,
and when he had admitted defeat she would insist on having her own room. Then when Mark came—*if* he came...

Deep in her uneasy thoughts, she stumbled and would
have fallen if Thorn hadn't caught her arm. Jerked back to
the present, she realised that they were on a rough path,
overhung with climbing plants and luxuriant vegetation,
which led down to the shore.

As they reached it the huge, glowing orange disk of the sun slid into the sea and dusk fell, as it did in the near-Tropics, with the swiftness of a blue velvet theatre curtain swishing down.

When they left the path the heels on Lisa's sandals sank into the loose sand, making walking difficult.

"Why don't you take them off?" Thorn suggested, and when she did, one hand propping herself against the smooth, scaly trunk of a palm, he bent to remove his own sneakers.

Leaving their footwear, they began to walk, side by side but not touching. "I used to swim here as a child," he told her. "It's a marvellous place for water sports, with some of the best snorkelling and diving in North America."

The sand was warm and sensuous beneath her bare feet, waves whispered in to make lacy patterns on the gently sloping beach, while overhead the palm-fronds rustled in the balmy night breeze and stars began to twinkle.

It was beautiful and romantic, and suddenly she wanted to weep, to put her head down on her arms and cry her heart out. If only things were different. If only he *really* loved her...

But they weren't. And he didn't.

Knowing that, there was *no way* she would willingly make this a real marriage.

Earlier he had sounded infuriatingly confident of his own powers of persuasion, yet now he was making no attempt to take advantage of the idyllic tropical night to coax her into the right mood.

But he was a brilliant strategist... Perhaps his casual talk and pleasantly platonic manner were just a ploy to lull her into a false sense of security? To make her relax her guard before he moved in with the soft seduction?

Well, she was on guard and wary, so he was wasting his time...

"You're looking very fierce." His amused voice penetrated her thoughts, and with a start she realised that they had come to the end of the beach.

Ahead of them, beyond a low outcrop of coral rock and silhouetted against a full moon, a dark mass of mangroves were paddling at the water's edge.

The star-spangled sky was indigo and the placid sea gleamed black and silver. Apart from a few lights in the far distance they could have had the world to themselves. It was a magic night—a night made for lovers...

Dropping down, Thorn patted the fine, smooth sand invitingly and said, "Come and sit beside me and tell me *why* you're looking so fierce."

So now he was going to beguile her, spread his charm as thick as butter on the Sunday crumpets, entice and seduce her with honeyed words...

Like hell he was! "I'd rather not," she said coolly, preparing to move away.

The next second his fingers closed around her ankle and she was jerked off balance and tumbled into his lap. One arm holding her, his voice dripping with satisfaction, he said, "That's better. I don't like it when you're standoffish."

She could feel his firm thighs beneath her buttocks, and one of her arms was pressed against his muscular chest. Though her heart began to race uncomfortably at the contact, some warning sixth sense urged her to remain quite still.

"Let me go," she said tightly.

"You don't really want me to let you go." His voice was deliberately taunting and his white teeth gleamed in a derisive smile. "You're just saying that to try and save your foolish pride..."

Where was the charm, the honeyed words?

"…but it's a waste of time. I know you're mad about me and—"

"What on earth makes you think I'm mad about you?" she broke in, somehow managing to keep her voice cool and disdainful.

"Being the kind of woman you are, you wouldn't have married me if you weren't."

Shaken to the core, Lisa snapped, "Ever heard of sexual attraction? And that died as soon as I found out just what kind of man you are."

He laughed jeeringly. "Don't give me that. You're infatuated and you know it. If I hadn't had other plans and I'd really turned on the heat you'd have jumped into my bed that very first night."

"Why, you conceited, egotistical…" She tried to struggle free, but he held her easily with one arm.

"It will suit me very nicely to have an eager young wife, and if you're obedient I'll even be kind to you…in my fashion," he added cynically.

His free hand moved to cup her breast, handling it with studied insolence. The nipple firmed beneath his touch and he laughed softly. "Your body's reactions are very passionate and unbridled. I wonder, when you've served your purpose and I want to get rid of you, will they make you come begging to my feet?"

"You bastard…" His sneering words and the open contempt in his voice made Lisa see red. Her control snapped and, sobbing with rage, she went for him like a tigress, striking at his mocking face with a kind of primitive savagery that she hadn't known she was capable of.

The fury of her first onslaught knocked him backwards. Making no attempt to retaliate, he fended her off until her flailing fist caught him a crack on the cheek-bone, then, grasping her wrists, he rolled over and, pinning her arms above her head, used the weight of his body to stop her thrashing about.

A second later his mouth found hers, the pressure of his kiss forcing her head back against the sand.

Senses reeling, physically and emotionally drained, she lay limp until into the vacuum left by spent anger another sensation started to flow—*desire*. It came rolling in in molten waves and she was filled with an overwhelming need for this man, her mouth opening beneath his as a flower opened to the sun.

His searching tongue, the slight rasp of his stubble against her jaw, the weight of his body on hers were potent aphrodisiacs.

He released her wrists, and while he explored her mouth she ran her fingers into his tumbled black hair, learning the shape of his skull and the strength of his neck muscles, the way his hair, surprisingly silky, curled a little into his nape.

Moving downwards, leaving a trail of fire in its wake, his hand brushed the side of her breast and followed the curves of her waist, hip and thigh.

Suddenly her clothes were a barrier. She wanted desperately to feel his touch on her flesh. As though she'd spoken the longing aloud, swiftly and deftly he undid the buttons of her short jacket and dealt with the front fastening of her bra.

When his lean fingers stroked over her ribcage and breasts and found the firm thrust of her nipples she moaned. A second or so later his mouth took the place of his fingers, and she jerked and shuddered with desire as he teased and suckled, sending the most exquisite sensations running through her.

She was making little whimpering noises deep in her throat when, unbuttoning her skirt, he spread it on the sand and swiftly divested them both of their remaining clothing. When he returned to her, with a kind of awe she felt the hard maleness of him against the heated sensitivity of her skin.

"Please...please..." she begged.

He parted her thighs, and his fingers moved lightly but surely on a voyage of discovery, before he made the first slow, careful entry.

In the moment of complete stillness that followed he whispered, "All right, darling?"

Her throat dry with fire, she croaked, "Yes...oh, yes..."

Then he was moving again, deeply, rhythmically, while the wonderful sensations he was engendering spiralled and grew in intensity until her whole being was transfixed.

For a second or two he paused, deliberately keeping her waiting, before, with a deep, powerful thrust, he released her. She cried out as the whole world seemed to explode in a rain of fireworks and her body convulsed beneath his.

Her reaction triggered his own, and a second or two later, his breath coming harshly, he shuddered into stillness and his head dropped to lie heavily on her breast.

Aware of nothing but her own body and the weight of Thorn's, Lisa lay blind and deaf while delicious waves of release spread from a central core through her entire being.

Gradually consciousness of the outside world crept back. She could hear the play of the warm breeze through the palms, the gentle shush of the waves and, somewhere close at hand, the call of a night bird.

She gave an involuntary sigh, and Thorn stirred and lifted his head. Feeling the movement, she opened her eyes and found him looking down at her in the moonlight.

She was unaware that she'd been crying until, with his thumbs, he wiped away her tears, on his dark face an expression that was a combination of joy and tenderness. Though he had hoped for an ardent response, he had been both delighted and astounded by the depth of her passion.

"Enjoy your first time?" he asked softly.

"Yes." It was such an understatement that she wanted to laugh. Her defences non-existent at that moment, she admitted, "I had no idea feelings could be so...*intense*. I thought I was going to die."

There was a gleam of triumph in his eyes that she couldn't at that moment bring herself to resent, and she saw his white teeth gleam in a smile before he asked wickedly, "Didn't you know that extremes of sensation heighten one another?"

It took a moment or two to sink in, then she realised the truth. Wanting to sound indignant, but only managing to sound wondering, she said, "You did it deliberately..."

"Did what?" He feigned innocence.

"Said all those horrible, humiliating things just to make me angry."

"I decided it was the best way to get through your defences," he admitted, "and making you furious served a double purpose. But I didn't expect you to be quite such a little hell-cat." He touched his cheek gingerly. "You nearly gave me a black eye. Aren't you sorry?"

Still in a state of euphoria bordering on intoxication, Lisa clasped her fingers behind his neck and, pulling his dark head down until his lips almost touched hers, whispered, "Just for the moment I can't be sorry about anything—"

His mouth stopped any further words as, with skill and a growing ardour, he set out to arouse her again. He was gentle in coaxing her body, steely in controlling his own, and soon she had abandoned herself and was responding with all the fervour of her passionate nature.

This time his lovemaking was leisurely. He moved maddeningly slowly, drawing shuddering breaths from her as he withdrew to the very tip before pressing inexorably back again.

Only when he knew that she was on the brink did he drive deeper and faster, holding himself back until she cried out and he felt the rhythmic pulsing deep inside her. Then, relaxing his control, he followed her into the abyss.

Afterwards, her skirt crumpled beneath them, she fell asleep in his arms, her head cradled on his chest, his chin on her silky curls.

A series of butterfly kisses made her sigh and stir.

"Wake up, darling," he said. "It's time we went back to bed. The air will get considerably cooler towards morning and I don't want you to take a chill."

But, too far under to fight her way to the surface, she mumbled something unintelligible and snuggled into his arms once more.

Lisa awakened slowly, indolently, and stretched, her mind still dazed with sleep but vaguely aware of a sense of bodily well-being and satisfaction.

She lay with her eyes closed while random thoughts began to filter into her consciousness. Today was going to be her wedding day… No, *yesterday* had been her wedding day… Mark hadn't made it back in time… But she remembered Thorn putting the ring on her finger, and afterwards Mrs Kirk's cake and the helicopter flight to Jacob's Island—

Suddenly the trickle of thoughts turned into a deluge as the dam burst. Swamped with a terrible hurt and a kind of bitter, futile anger, she remembered Thorn's perfidy, and then, with searing self-contempt and loathing, her own helpless surrender.

As though to deliberately torture her, her mind replayed the scene on the beach. Once more she could feel the ecstasy as his body invaded and dominated hers, the warm evening air cool against her flushed face, the graininess of the sand beneath her head…

But now, though she had no recollection of coming back to the house, her head rested on a plump pillow and she was lying not on her own crumpled skirt but in a comfortable bed.

With a half-stifled groan, she opened her eyes to see broad daylight filling the room and what appeared to be a fine, bright day outside.

Turning her head a little, she found that Thorn was beside her. Propped on one elbow, he was studying her face as though memorising every feature—the mouth that was a shade too wide for the delicate, heart-shaped face, the high cheek-bones and dimpled chin, the straight nose that stopped just short of classical elegance, the almond eyes with the intriguing upward tilt at the outer corners, the flawless skin with its golden tan...

"Good morning." He smiled down at her.

Even though she bitterly resented her own subjection, she found herself thinking how devastatingly attractive he looked, how sexy and masculine, with his brilliant, thickly lashed green-gold eyes, a lock of black hair falling over his forehead and a dark growth of stubble adorning his jaw and upper lip.

He bent to kiss her, but, gathering all her strength, she turned her head away and his lips brushed across her averted cheek. "No morning kiss?" he enquired quizzically.

"You must think I'm a pushover," she muttered.

"I think you're enchanting." And it was the truth. Though she wasn't his usual type at all—he liked tall, sophisticated, raven-haired beauties who knew the score— he'd become strangely fascinated by her. She had courage and warmth and sweetness, and a sexual aura of which she seemed totally unaware.

Gritting her teeth, she informed him, "And I think *you're* a lying, devious swine."

Sighing, he admitted, "I had hoped that after last night things might run smoothly, that today you might feel a little more…shall we say *resigned* to the thought of being my wife, a little more cheerful?"

"I feel awful," she said flatly.

"Would an early-morning cup of tea improve matters?"

When she made no answer he got out of bed and, pulling on a short, navy blue silk robe, padded barefoot to the door.

Watching him go, she wished fervently that she would never have to set eyes on him again. She wanted to run and keep running until she had left all memory of him far behind. But that, she knew quite well, was impossible. While ever she drew breath she would remember him and his lovemaking.

He had proved to be a superb lover, accomplished and skilful, but then, she thought cynically, she would have expected that.

What she *hadn't* expected was the care and consideration he'd shown, the determination not to hurt her…*physically* at least.

He'd been heart-breakingly tender with her body, but he hadn't cared in the slightest how much he'd hurt her *mentally*. And though he might have cause to hate Mark *she* was just an innocent victim.

Still he'd lied and cheated and deceived her, set out to make her love him, and pretended to love her. He'd swept her into a travesty of marriage and then, for his own ends and in spite of her opposition, had employed despicable methods to consummate that marriage.

In some ways it would have been easier if he'd simply used force to get his way. At least that would have kept her pride intact. She could have blamed him and absolved herself.

Now, no matter how she tried to escape the fact, she only had herself to blame. It was her own body that had betrayed her. Feeling cheap and degraded, she loathed and despised herself. Knowing exactly how things stood, how *could* she have given in to him so easily?

But, having made that mistake, she had no intention of repeating it. If he thought that, having once surrendered to him, she would continue to do so, he had another think coming! His sexual magnetism wasn't as irresistible as he seemed to imagine.

She would stay in control and steer clear of any further involvement. And then if Mark did come she would leave with him…

The door opened to admit Thorn, carrying a tray of tea and biscuits. Lisa sat up abruptly, pushing back her dishevelled curls. Finding that she was naked except for the betrothal pendant he had given her, she pulled the sheet high across her chest and trapped it beneath her arms.

Putting the tray on the bedside cabinet, he eyed the sheet anchored across her breasts with open mockery.

Oh, why hadn't she got up and dressed while she had the chance, instead of lying here indulging in futile regrets?

Making no comment, however, he poured tea for them both and passed her a cup. Her throat desert-dry, she began to sip it gratefully. When he offered her a biscuit she shook her head.

Sitting on the edge of the bed, he said sardonically, "Don't tell me that, as well as generating a belated maidenly modesty, your first encounter with love has deprived you of speech?"

"That wasn't *love*," she objected bitterly. "That was just lust."

He shrugged. "Whatever you care to call it you seem to have a natural affinity for it."

She flushed hotly. Her first real encounter with physical love had surprised and shocked her. She had never fully appreciated what a tempestuous nature lay buried beneath her normal everyday calm. Thrown into the turbulent sea of passion, she had found herself at home, swimming like a fish.

To stave off any further mocking comments, she asked hurriedly, "How did I get back here? The last thing I remember is being on the beach."

"You were fast asleep, so I carried you."

"All that way?" she exclaimed.

"There's a short cut, and you're not heavy."

Uncomfortably she muttered, "I don't know why I didn't waken."

"You were absolutely shattered. But that's not surprising." His voice deepened. "When I made love to you you were so ardent, so passionate…"

She bent her head, her face showing all too clearly her feelings of shame and humiliation.

"Don't look like that," he ordered abruptly.

She swallowed. "Like what?"

"Like you're giving yourself hell for being a warm, responsive woman. Like you hate yourself."

"I loathe myself…even more than I loathe *you*," she added recklessly, and saw the gleam of anger in his heavy-lidded eyes.

Almost immediately, however, a shutter came down, hiding all expression. After a second or two, putting his empty cup back on the tray, Thorn suggested with smooth politeness, "Would you care to join me in a swim before breakfast?"

Intending to refuse curtly, she changed her mind. If Mark *did* come, it might be a day or two before he arrived, and in the meantime—the very thought made shivers run through her—she was trapped here with Thorn. Common sense insisted that it was bound to make things easier if she could defuse the situation and get back, as near as possible, onto a normal, everyday footing.

Once that was achieved, all she had to do was stay cool

and in control and keep their relationship as civilised as possible.

Forcing herself to speak lightly, she said, ''That sounds nice, but I feel grubby and I've still got sand in my hair...'' Trying to ignore the quick, reminiscent smile that curved his lips and brought a blush to her cheeks, she forged on, ''So I'd like to shower first.''

''My own feelings exactly.''

So why didn't he go and do it? she thought exasperatedly. With him there and no robe handy she couldn't bring herself to get out of bed.

When she failed to make a move he asked, ''Are you waiting for an invitation to share my bathroom? Or are you shy?''

''Neither,'' she answered untruthfully.

''Well, in that case—'' he got to his feet and with one fluid movement twitched back the light covering of bedclothes, leaving her naked and vulnerable ''—out you get.''

Reminding herself that he'd seen her bare before, and unwilling to scuttle for the bathroom like a frightened rabbit, she got out of bed with what dignity she could muster and walked over to her wardrobe.

Without consciously thinking it out, the decision had been made and was firm in her mind. She was *not* going to wear anything that Thorn had bought for her, and that included her rings and the betrothal pendant—especially the pendant, with its clasped hands and lovers kissing, which made a complete mockery of their relationship.

Silently thanking Mrs Kirk for packing all the things she'd brought from England, she began to search through the garments on the top shelf. By the time she had located what she was looking for, to her relief Thorn had disappeared into his own bathroom.

She unfastened the pendant and dropped that and her engagement ring onto Thorn's chest of drawers, but when it came to removing her wedding ring she hesitated, feeling a peculiar reluctance.

Perhaps because it had been put on in church? Because then she had believed that Thorn loved her, that this was to be a real marriage?

Whatever the reason, she couldn't bring herself to take it off. Calling herself all kinds of a fool, she left it where it was, with the proviso that she'd give it back to him before she left the island.

After she'd cleaned her teeth she showered, letting the warm water cascade down a body that bore the traces of his passion—a body that felt *different*, sleek and glowing and fulfilled, even though her thoughts were painful and agitated.

How strange that her mind and body, which until recently she'd always thought of as a harmonising whole, could be so at variance.

Sighing, she washed her hair, rinsing out the last grains of sand before fastening a towel turban-wise around her head then putting on flat sandals and the yellow swimsuit she'd had since the fifth form. Old and tight, pulling across the bust, it was far from flattering, but that suited her very well. The last thing she wanted to do was rouse his ardour.

She was in the bedroom, trying to find a clip to fasten her hair into a pony-tail, when Thorn came back carrying a couple of beach towels. Showered and shaved, dressed in sandals and black swimming trunks that hugged his lean hips, he looked disturbingly masculine and virile.

His eyes running the length of her slender body, he demanded, "What the *hell* are you wearing?"

She looked at him with cool disdain until her dignity was spoiled by the turban slipping drunkenly over one ear. Pulling it off, letting the long, damp curls tumble over her bare shoulders, she said, "I don't know what you mean."

"You know perfectly well what I mean." Going to her

wardrobe, he searched until he found the set of swimwear he'd bought for her. "Stop playing silly games and put this on."

"I'm not playing, and I won't put it on." Her earlier resolve to keep things cool and civilised went by the board. "I've no intention of wearing any of the things you bought for me. You never meant this to be a real marriage and I refuse to be treated like a—"

All at once he was looming over her, his free hand holding her jaw between thumb and spread fingers, lifting her face for his merciless scrutiny, leaving her no place to hide.

"You'll be treated exactly how I want to treat you." His voice was dangerously quiet, and the look in his eyes made her start to tremble. "If you're amenable then I'll be kind. But if you fight me you'll have to take the consequences.

"Now for the last time, Lisa, are you taking this thing off willingly, or do I have to rip it off you?"

As she hesitated, trying to drum up the courage to defy him, he added softly, "I'm warning you, if it's the latter I might well be tempted to take my exercise in a more exciting way than swimming…"

CHAPTER EIGHT

ONLY too aware that the threat was no idle one, Lisa jerked free and, snatching the swimwear from Thorn's hand, fled into the bathroom, tears of anger and frustration filling her eyes.

He was an overbearing, arrogant, domineering brute! She would have dearly loved to defy him, but unwillingly she acknowledged that he had the power to make her do as he wished, so for the next few days at least she was going to have to grin and bear it.

When reluctantly she returned wearing the leopard-spotted bikini, ignoring her mutinous expression, he said with infuriating satisfaction, "That's better."

"Power must be addictive," she remarked bitterly.

"Oh, it is," he agreed. "Once you've developed a taste for it everything else seems bland and boring in comparison."

A gleam in his eye that told her he was deliberately baiting her, he added, "Now come and give me a kiss to prove what a docile little wife you're going to be."

Being treated with such studied mockery riled her and made it hard to kowtow to him, but somehow she forced herself to move closer and, standing on tiptoe, brush cool lips across his cheek.

He sighed. "Hardly enthusiastic, but still, it's a start. Come on, then, let's go." Throwing the towels over one shoulder, he took her hand. Biting her lip, she forbore to pull it away.

Outside, although early, it was already hot and sunny, a stiffish breeze hustling white cotton-wool clouds across the blue sky and making the seagulls wheel in flight.

Angry thoughts seething in her mind, Lisa scarcely noticed. It was one thing to *tell* herself that all she had to do was stay cool and in control but quite another to actually do it. And as for keeping their relationship *civilised*, how could she when he behaved like a barbarian?

Without speaking, they followed the short cut down to the beach where sparkling waves creamed onto the sand and palm-fronds tossed in the warm, tropical wind. In the shallows the water was a pale aquamarine while further out it deepened to peacock-blue and lapis lazuli and, by the reef, the most wonderful shade of jade.

Near the mainland bright sailboards were dotted about, and several fishing boats were heading away from the keys. Closer, the white sails of some dinghies billowed and filled, sending the small craft scudding over the glittering sea.

Thorn dropped the towels on the sand; having slipped off their sandals, still hand in hand, they waded in and took the plunge.

Lisa gasped at the momentary shock of cold water against heated flesh, then, as she adjusted to it, it flowed around her, sensuous as warm silk. Though swimming in the sea was new to her, the knowledge that Thorn was by her side gave her confidence.

Doing a leisurely breast-stroke, she was able to peer down through the clear water and discover a new and magical world, catching glimpses of living coral, gently swaying anemones, and fantastically coloured fish darting about the underwater garden that clothed the seabed.

Though Thorn was a much stronger swimmer he stayed with her, and, as soon as she began to tire, stopped to tread water while, arms spread, she floated on her back, her long hair drifting around her face like a mermaid's tresses.

Twisting her head a little, she saw that his eyes were travelling the length of her slender body. His intense expression set alarm bells ringing and made her heart pick up speed. Suddenly agitated, apprehensive, she turned from her back onto her side to strike out for the beach.

Reaching out a strong hand, Thorn grasped her wrist. She began to struggle, and coughed as she swallowed some salt water.

"Don't," he said sharply, and one hand moved to cup her chin. His touch was command enough, his size and strength at once a threat and a reassurance.

He supported her head while his other hand pushed her bikini-top down to free her breasts before he drew her closer. Her nipples grazed the dark hair on his chest and went instantly, achingly erect.

His hand spread across her buttocks, he pressed the lower half of her body to his, and she felt his hard male need in a way that made her stomach clench with desire.

"Put your arms around my neck," he commanded huskily.

Like someone with no will of her own she obeyed, and his hands slid down her legs to guide them into place around his waist. When they were locked around him he spread his hands and arms across her back to imprison her there.

While the swell moving shorewards made their clinging bodies rise and fall she gazed at him helplessly and felt a bitter-sweet pain—a pain that held him at its very core, a pain that, while it crucified her, gave her immeasurable joy.

Then his mouth was on hers, and while he supported her body with the tenderness of a parent supporting a child he ravaged her mouth with all the ferocity of a conqueror.

Releasing her lips at last, he ducked his head and, one

after another, found her nipples, setting up answering spasms deep within her.

She drew long, shuddering breaths and, unable to help herself, pressed his wet head to her breast, wanting to prolong this exquisite torment.

After a while he raised his head to whisper, "You want me. Tell me you want me."

Reluctant to admit it, she averted her face.

"Say it," he ordered. "I want to hear you say it."

"You know I do." Then, in a cry from the heart, she added, "But oh, God, I wish I didn't. I despise myself for wanting a man I hate—a man who's only using me."

She heard the hiss of breath being drawn through clenched teeth, and beneath the tan his face paled as though the words had been a handful of rocks she'd thrown at him.

Without another word he released her and turned to strike out for the beach. For a second or two she floundered before, gathering herself, she started to swim after him.

She was more tired than she'd realised and her arms felt as heavy as lead. The shore looked a long way away; little wavelets slapped spitefully in her face, and instead of buoying her up the sea seemed to be dragging her down.

Afraid of being left too far behind, she made a panicky effort to catch up. But almost at once iron bars tightened around her chest and her lungs began to labour. Gasping for breath, she swallowed a mouthful of water and, choking helplessly, went under.

Heart pounding, a roaring in her ears, she somehow fought her way to the surface, but before she could take a breath she was sinking again.

Then, miraculously, strong hands were holding her, keeping her head above water while she clutched wildly at him, gulping in air.

"Don't struggle," Thorn ordered sharply. Then, in a

quiet, measured voice, he said, "I've got you safe. Just turn onto your back."

Trusting him implicitly, she used will-power like a whip to force herself to go limp and float. Getting behind her, he turned on his back and, a hand beneath her chin, his body half supporting hers, kicked out for the shore. When they reached the shallows he stopped swimming and, finding his feet, lifted her high in his arms and carried her up the beach.

Putting her on the warm sand, he went down on his knees beside her.

"Thank you," she managed hoarsely, her breath still coming in ragged gasps. "I'm afraid I'm not much of a swimmer."

"I should never have left you." He sounded angry, but she guessed that that anger was directed against himself. Then he asked urgently, "Are you all right? Did you swallow much water?"

"I'm fine. I swallowed a little, that's all." But suddenly, despite the warmth of the sand, she was cold to the marrow and shaking, trembling in every limb.

His face tightening with concern, Thorn said, "Let's get you back."

Her bikini-top was hanging wetly around her waist and she made a fumbling attempt to pull it up.

"Leave that," he ordered brusquely. Wrapping the towels around her, he gathered her close and, cradling her against his muscular chest, set off at a pace that proved his superb fitness and stamina.

Looking at his grim face, wanting to ease the tension she saw there, Lisa made an effort and joked through chattering teeth, "If you're n-not careful this is g-going to develop into a habit."

He gave her a quick, startled glance, then, with a lop-sided smile, said, "I can think of more onerous ones."

When they reached the house he carried her straight up-stairs and into the bathroom. Putting her down on a stool, he turned on the taps and poured in some creamy lotion. "A hot bath is what you need."

The instant it was full he urged her to her feet and, while she stood like a child under his ministrations, unwrapped the towels, stripped off her wet bikini and helped her in.

She leaned back against the sloping end, and as the scented water lapped around her a comforting warmth began to replace the inner chill and she stopped shaking.

Watching the colour start to creep back into her face, he asked, "OK to be left for a couple of minutes?"

"Of course."

"There's no 'of course' about it; shock's a funny thing."

Grateful for his concern, Lisa insisted, "I'm fine now, really." And, the numbing coldness passing, she *was* feeling practically herself again. After another look to reassure himself, he departed.

He seemed to be back almost at once. "Drink this."

Sitting up, she accepted the cup of hot, sweet tea, and, though she *hated* sweet tea, sipped obediently.

As soon as the cup was empty he took it from her and, brushing a damp curl away from her cheek with his fingertips, said, "Now relax, and in a little while you can have breakfast in bed."

"I don't need to go back to bed," she protested. "I'm not an invalid."

"You're going to spend at least the morning in bed." Sardonically, he added, "And, to save you worrying, I *do* mean alone... If you want company you'll have to ask for it."

When he'd gone she leaned her head against the curved headrest and closed her eyes. He was a strange mixture, she thought—caring and considerate in some ways, cold-hearted and callous in others.

But a man among men.

And if any woman could ever gain his respect and affection then she would be a very lucky woman indeed. To be loved by a man like him would be the greatest gift life could offer...

She was almost asleep by the time Thorn returned for the second time.

As she struggled upright he asked, "Have you rinsed your hair?"

"No."

He passed her the hand spray and, when she'd rinsed the salt from her tangle of brown curls, took a towel and rubbed them almost dry.

A moment later he was unfolding a bath sheet. "Let's have you out."

"I can manage by myself..."

Ignoring her protest, he wrapped the sheet around her and lifted her out as though she weighed no more than a feather. Then, with a thoroughness and care that heated her blood and made every nerve-ending in her body tingle into life, she was dried and powdered.

A few minutes later, wearing a thigh-length T-shirt, her hair brushed into a silky mass, she was back in bed, propped up against soft pillows, flushed and aroused.

Judging by Thorn's ironic eyes, as he helped her to hot waffles and maple syrup he knew exactly what he'd done to her, and he'd enjoyed doing it.

But of course! The previous night he'd made the point that extremes of sensation heightened one another... And, just now, he'd said that if she wanted company she'd have to ask for it. Obviously he was hoping that her earlier fright would break down the barriers as last night's anger had done, and drive her into his arms.

Well, his plan had failed. Even though part of her wanted *desperately* to turn to him, she wouldn't allow herself to.

Watching him surreptitiously from beneath long lashes, Lisa soon came to realise that in deliberately arousing her he had become hoist with his own petard. Serve him right, she thought maliciously. Still, the knowledge did nothing to calm her own excitement.

She ate without actually tasting a thing, and as soon as she'd emptied her plate and finished the coffee he'd poured her, nervous in case he should change his mind and even more nervous that she might change hers, she faked a yawn.

"Tired?" His green eyes glinted.

Unable to trust her voice, she nodded.

He gave her a wry little salute, tacitly acknowledging her victory, before settling her down as though she were a child.

Leaving the windows wide open, he drew the curtains against the brightness and said softly, "Have a good sleep." A moment later the door clicked to behind him.

The warm breeze billowed the pale, flower-sprigged curtains, a light plane droned overhead, and in the distance gulls cried harshly...

Her body still aroused, she hadn't expected to sleep, but in just a moment or two consciousness faded and her eyelids drooped...

As gradually Lisa emerged from a deep sleep into a more shallow one she began to dream. Someone was lying beside her, kissing her—soft, teasing kisses on her face and closed eyelids—while skilful hands slipped beneath the thin cotton T-shirt to stroke and coax her breasts into eager life.

Sighing, she abandoned herself completely, and when those tantalising lips brushed hers and would have moved away her arms went around a warm neck and her own lips parted enticingly.

Eyes shut tight, she savoured to the full the enjoyment which those unhurried lips and hands were bestowing—and receiving—as they kissed and caressed her into a yielding mass of sensations.

Moving to accommodate the knowing, intrusive fingers, giving little murmurs of pleasure as they reached the very heart of those exquisite sensations, she waited for them to bring her to a breathtaking climax.

But maddeningly they stopped short and withdrew, refusing to give her the satisfaction she craved... And then, unbelievably, he was moving away.

With a whimper of frustration she tried to pull him down to her. No dream lover, this but a man of flesh and blood, he held back.

"You'll have to *ask*, Lisa..." The mocking whisper was close to her ear.

She wanted to tell him that she had no intention of asking, but she found herself unable to say the words, incapable of breaking the dark enchantment of her senses, incapable of denying the hunger that filled her.

"Please...oh, please..."

After an endless moment she felt his now familiar weight as, bare flesh against bare flesh, he fitted himself into the waiting cradle of her hips.

His first deep thrust made her body clench in ecstasy and started the tightening spiral that was to culminate in a shattering explosion of light and joy.

After a moment or two Thorn rolled onto his back and gathered her to him. In the aftermath of their love-making she lay quietly, her head on his shoulder, while the world righted itself and their heartbeats and breathing slowly returned to normal.

Soon she would hate both herself and him, but at that moment all she could feel was delight in the virility and strength of this man who was her husband, delight in the pleasure they could give each other. Because this was an *exchange* of pleasure, a giving and receiving on both sides; of that she had no doubt.

And it was wonderful that it should be so.

Sighing, she moved the hand that was lying palm down on his chest, and her fingers enjoyed the crisp yet silky scattering of hair.

Thorn turned his head, and her eyes opened to find that he was smiling down at her, on his dark face a combination of triumph and mockery and a kind of tenderness.

Lisa was starting to smile back when the first cold breath of returning sanity made her remember that there was no love between them. It was merely *sex*...

She didn't realise that she'd spoken the last four words aloud until, brushing a curl away from her flushed cheek, he said softly, "There's nothing wrong with sex so long as it's a joyful experience for both partners. If you stop fighting not only me but your own inclinations and enjoy what we have together you won't find the situation too hard to bear."

His casual words made Lisa stiffen. If he was expecting her to stay docilely with him until, his revenge completed, he was ready to let her go, he was wrong.

She pulled away sharply and sat up against the tumbled pillows. "And I won't mind that you gulled me into this marriage? That you're only using me to try and hurt my brother? That when you've achieved your ends you'll get rid of me just as ruthlessly?"

He sat up too and, throwing a bare, muscular arm around her shoulders, clamped her to his side. When she strained away angrily, averting her head, he took her chin in his free hand and turned her face to his.

A cruel little twist to his mouth, he said, "Providing you play your cards right I may not want to get rid of you. If at the end of five months I find I—"

Seething with anger and resentment, she broke in, "Why five months?"

"That's how long Ginny's marriage lasted," Thorn said harshly. "How long it took him to drive her into taking drugs…"

Shivering, Lisa found herself wondering exactly what kind of man her brother was. She didn't know the rights and wrongs of his brief marriage so she was unable to defend him. But what little she knew of him personally—his letters and his kindness to *her* pointed to him being thoughtful and caring, not the type to ill-treat his young, pregnant wife…

"But as I was saying," Thorn went on more smoothly, his thumb moving caressingly over her jaw, "if at the end of that time I find I still want you, I intend to let our marriage go on."

She clenched her hands until her nails bit painfully into the soft palms before she was able to say sweetly, "Really, you're *too* kind. You've just overlooked one thing."

He raised a black brow enquiringly. "And what's that?"

"*Me.* What *I* want. What *I* intend to do."

Smiling slightly, he shook his head. "Perhaps it's time you got one thing straight. You'll do exactly what I tell you to do. Though I propose to be a tolerant husband, my plans don't include—"

Her teeth snapped together. "Perhaps it's time *you* got one thing straight. Your plans, whatever they are, are all washed up. I don't intend to stay with you for five *days* if I can help it, let alone five months. If Mark *does* come—"

"He'll come."

"Then I'm going to leave with him!"

Thorn's grip on her chin tightened just a fraction. "I'm afraid I can't allow you to do that."

"You can't stop me."

Brave words, but if it came to a confrontation between

the two men… Shivering, she tried not to think what might happen. The prospect of being fought over like a bone between two snarling dogs was a terrifying one.

Apparently telepathic, Thorn said calmly, ''If you care in the slightest for your brother, that kind of unpleasantness won't be necessary. With some co-operation from you there can be a more civilised but none the less effective outcome.''

Wide hazel eyes fixed on his face, Lisa waited, her heart thumping against her ribcage.

''At the moment he still has some resources and the semblance of a normal life left. I *could* hold off, financially speaking, and though Landers Holdings own his firm I *could* stand back and allow him to keep running it.

''On the other hand—'' the green eyes were as cold as glacial ice ''—I have enough power to bankrupt him. I could have him out on the street without a cent by tomorrow… It's up to you.''

Somehow she fought back. ''If he's the sort of brute you say he is, why should I care what happens to him?''

Thorn's challenge was cool and calculated. ''But you *don't* believe he is, do you?''

No, she didn't believe it. The answer was waiting in her subconscious. With that same sure instinct which had insisted that something was wrong with Thorn's proposal she was convinced that things *couldn't* be as he'd painted them.

Yet there was no doubt that *he* believed they were. So could he be mistaken?

Carefully she said, ''Some time ago you told me that Mark was planning to give me a sum of money. Was that the truth?''

''Yes. No doubt at that stage he thought he could afford to. But you don't care about the money.'' It was a statement, not a question.

Still she answered it. ''No, I don't care about the money.

But doesn't the fact that he planned to give it to me prove that he isn't the kind of man you think he is?''

''Though it would serve my purpose better if you believed in Mark, in all fairness I have to point out that a lot of men who ill-treat their wives are generous in other ways.''

When she remained silent, green eyes holding golden-hazel ones, he asked, ''So which is it to be, Lisa? I'll break him if I have to, but it would be a more fitting punishment to let him sweat over you as I sweated over Ginny.''

Only one thing was clear in her mind: she *couldn't* stand by and see Mark ruined. He'd shown her nothing but kindness and he *was* her brother.

If she agreed to stay it would at least give him a few months' breathing-space, and, though the two men hated and mistrusted one another, hopefully he wouldn't worry about her as much as Thorn seemed to think…

Reading her decision in her expressive face, he smiled and said, ''I'm glad you've decided to co-operate.''

Trying to hold onto some shred of control, she shook her head. ''You're going much too fast. If I stay with you I want my own room and your promise not to—''

His hand moved over her lips, stopping the words. ''I'm allowing no strings, Lisa. If you stay with me it will be on *my* terms.''

''Utter subjugation, you mean!''

His index finger traced the passionate outline of her mouth. ''You might find you enjoy it.''

''Like hell!''

He laughed. ''Well, if it's *equality* you want you can make a bid for it right now…''

Thrown as much by the look in his eyes as his words, she said uncertainly, ''I don't understand what you mean.''

''Then I'll show you.'' Leaning towards her, he brushed

his lips lightly across hers while she sat quite still. Drawing back a little, he commanded softly, "Now you kiss me."

She looked at his sculptured mouth and felt a constriction in her throat.

"Kiss me," he urged. "Despite everything, you know you want to."

It was the truth. She did want to. Like someone under a spell she touched her mouth to his. When his lips stayed disappointingly closed she ran the tip of her tongue along them and heard his slight gasp before they opened beneath hers and he deepened the kiss.

Thrilled with her little victory, she took a second or two to register that his hands had slipped beneath her T-shirt and were spanning her slim waist.

Then he was sliding down the bed, taking her with him so that her body was sprawled half across his.

One of his hands caught and held hers, carrying it to lie over his heart, trapping it there while he whispered, "Go on, touch me."

Her eyes closed tight, she obeyed, letting her fingers move over his hair-roughened chest in a tactile exploration as erotic as it was satisfying.

She'd always wanted to touch him freely, and now she delighted in discovering the solid bone and muscle, the smooth skin and powerful curve of shoulder and biceps, the leathery texture of the small, tight nipple.

Encouraged by his quickening heartbeat, her fingers travelled over the strong ribcage, the trim waist and lean hip to the taut flatness of his stomach.

As she stroked downwards to find and hold firm male flesh she heard his breathing grow ragged. Smiling with the age-old knowledge of Eve, she squeezed and caressed, triumphantly aware that she had a power over him that was almost as great as his over her.

Except that as far as he was concerned almost any woman would do.

The thought shocked and chilled her like a douche of icy cold water, halting her hand and making her freeze into stillness. But even as she tried to move away his arms were imprisoning her, his voice saying, "Oh, no, you don't, my dear little wife."

"Let me go." She began to struggle. "I don't want to—"

But the words were lost as he rolled over, pinning her beneath him, covering her mouth with his.

Unwilling to give in, for a while she resisted fiercely, fighting her own impulses as well as him. She hadn't the strength to stop him, she knew, but at least it would save her pride if, thinking she'd teased him deliberately, he was angry enough to just take her, to satisfy only himself.

He wasn't.

Nor was he a man to let her get away with what he must have regarded as deliberate provocation.

When, exhausted, she stopped fighting and tried passive resistance, with ruthless hands he stripped off the T-shirt, baring her breasts for his intimate attention. Using all his considerable skill and expertise, he slowly drove her wild, wringing from her little gasps and moans that she was unable to stifle.

But only when she was writhing beneath him, sobbing and pleading, racked with sensations so exquisite that they were almost torture, did he relent, and with a few powerful thrusts send her whirling through space to drift slowly back to earth.

Almost before his weight lifted from her she was asleep once more, physically and emotionally spent.

Lisa awoke to instant and complete remembrance. A combination of excitement and humiliation washing over her in heated waves, she glanced around. With relief she discovered that she was alone in the big bed and the room was empty.

Sighing, she freed herself from the tangled clothes and, stiff and aching in every limb, stumbled over to the window to draw back the curtains.

The early innocence of the day had given way to a brash afternoon—late afternoon, judging by the position of the sun.

If this had been the start of a genuine, loving honeymoon she could scarcely have spent more time in bed, she thought with a flash of wry humour.

When a lengthy shower had banished most of the aches and pains and eased her stiff muscles, a big, fluffy towel fastened sarong-wise above her breasts, she went to find fresh undies and a cotton skirt and top—looking specifically for the things she'd brought with her from England.

The only undies that remained in the drawer were the delicate scraps of gossamer that Thorn had bought for her. With a sudden, angry suspicion, she slid aside the wardrobe door. All her new clothes hung there, but her old ones had vanished.

She was still standing fuming helplessly when the door opened and Thorn strode in. There was an arrogant tilt to his dark head, a mixture of triumph and purposefulness in his manner. Casually dressed in light cotton trousers and a black sports shirt, his hair freshly combed, he looked fit and formidable. And unbearably smug.

"What have you done with my clothes?" she burst out.

"Disposed of them," he said calmly.

"Well, if you think I'm going to wear anything you've bought—" the towel slipped an inch or two and she grasped at it "—you've got another think coming."

He shrugged. "It's plenty warm enough; you shouldn't catch a chill, so whether you wear clothes or not is up to you. I much prefer you without them.'' Suddenly he was looming over her. ''But I'm afraid I must insist on you wearing these.''

Before she could stop him he'd lifted her left hand and slipped the engagement ring back on above her wedding band. But when he would have fastened the pendant around her neck, in a fit of rage at its mocking inappropriateness she tore it from his fingers and threw it across the room.

Standing quite still, his hard face wiped clear of all expression, he said softly, ''Pick it up, Lisa.''

''I won't.''

''You'll pick it up and wear it to please me.''

Desperately she fought back. ''If I obey your every command my life won't be my own.''

His eyes met and held hers, and she saw molten anger in their green-gold depths—an anger all the more deadly for being quiet, controlled. ''You'll obey me.''

Though he wasn't touching her and his voice was still soft, there was something about him—a kind of ruthless implacability— that scared her half to death.

Condemning herself as cowardly, not knowing that many a tough businessman had quailed beneath that look, she tried to hold out against him, to pit the force of her will against his. But his determination was so strong that she felt it start to bend hers as a strong man could bend an iron bar.

Suddenly it snapped, and with a half-sob she crossed the room and went down on her knees to feel under the chest of drawers for the pendant. When she'd retrieved it, her hands were shaking so much that she was unable to fasten the catch.

''Let me do that for you.'' His voice was a soft, satisfied purr.

When it hung round her neck, cold and heavy, gathering

the remains of her self-control around her like a tattered cloak, she said stiffly, "Thank you."

"A sweet pleasure," he returned mockingly.

She met his eyes, her own clouding with defiance. "'At a touch sweet pleasure melteth like to bubbles when rain pelteth...'" Mentally cocking a snook at him, she added, "At least my thoughts are my own."

Smiling, he quoted, "'O for a life of sensations rather than of thoughts!'" He added with a glint in his eye, "Keats always holds something appropriate."

"*Touché*," she said sardonically.

Little as she was, she had plenty of spirit, he conceded admiringly, and he was going to enjoy taming her. But first...

He glanced at his watch, then, his eyes travelling down the length of her slim, towel-clad body, he remarked idly, "It's a quarter after six. Are you intending to dress for dinner?"

A stubborn set to her chin, she said, "Not unless I can wear my own clothes."

"That's not possible, I'm afraid." He sounded almost regretful. "However, if you *want* to meet your brother wearing nothing but a towel..."

Her heart began to race with suffocating speed. "You don't mean he's coming now? This evening?"

With a quiet satisfaction that chilled her, Thorn confirmed, "He'll be here in a little over twenty minutes."

CHAPTER NINE

COLD dread suddenly lying like a lead weight in the pit of her stomach, Lisa asked sharply, "How do you know?"

"I've been in touch with the mainland."

"With your spies, you mean."

"How melodramatic," Thorn mocked.

"But you *did* have Mark followed?"

Coolly he admitted, "I don't like to leave anything to chance. Which is just as well. In the event, he's going to be here rather earlier than I'd anticipated." He went on sardonically, "So are you going to stay *déshabillé* and greet him with the news that your cruel husband has hidden the clothes you wanted to wear?"

Without deigning to answer, Lisa turned towards the wardrobe. Thorn's fingers closed round her wrist, stopping her in her tracks. "Just a reminder, darling," he said grimly. "If he tries to persuade you to leave with him, for *his* sake you'd better refuse." Then he added carelessly, "You can tell him *why* if you want to."

Oh, yes, she thought bitterly, that would serve your purpose nicely—make Mark carry an additional burden of guilt.

"You wouldn't like me to cry and cling to him just a little?" The words were out before she could stop them.

"Cry and cling to him all you want. But bear in mind that if he gets *too* concerned there could be consequences you might not care for…"

The spectre of two snarling dogs fighting over a bone came back to haunt her.

"So perhaps a slightly less dramatic approach might be more sensible. By all means tell him what a swine I am, how much you hate me for deceiving you. But don't leave him in any doubt that you intend to stay with me.

"If he cares about you at all—and I'm sure he does—his own imagination will put him on the rack."

With a cruel little smile, Thorn lifted the wrist he was imprisoning and touched his lips to the racing pulse before freeing it. A second later he had disappeared through the half-open door.

By the time she heard him start downstairs, her brain icy cold, her thoughts curiously sharp and lucid, Lisa had already decided on what seemed to be the only possible strategy.

Heart thumping, she slid into a low-cut sheath-dress in flame-coloured silk, with matching high-heeled sandals. Then, having twisted her hair into a knot of curls from which a few recalcitrant tendrils escaped, she applied make-up with care.

A glance in the cheval-glass confirmed that the naïve, vulnerable schoolgirl was gone. In her place was an elegant young woman who looked cool and self-assured, with a hoop of diamonds blazing on her finger and the pendant nestling just above the shadowy valley of her breasts.

All that was needed was a dab or two of the French perfume that she'd thought too sophisticated when Thorn had chosen it and she was ready.

He was in the living-room, standing by the French doors, which were thrown wide. Turning at her entrance, he did a double-take.

"Don't you like it?" she asked, adding innocently, "You chose it."

Recovering his aplomb, he said, "You look delightful."

But not at all what Mark would be expecting… It was as plain as if he'd spoken the words aloud, and she hugged herself.

Half expecting to hear the sound of an approaching helicopter, she queried, "How will Mark be getting here, do you know?"

"By boat." Thorn pointed, and through the lush vegetation Lisa caught a glimpse of a small blue motor boat lifting and falling slightly at its moorings.

"He's on his way up now." There was a savage satisfaction in Thorn's voice that told her only too clearly how much he was looking forward to the confrontation. But if she could play things down, refuse to make a melodrama of it…

Fighting to control her agitation, the panicky excitement, knowing that she must stay cool and composed at all costs, Lisa lifted her chin and went out onto the terrace.

When Thorn followed her she wanted to cheer. If only she could keep the initiative…

The earlier wind had dropped and now it was oppressively still, the very air seeming to be holding its breath. Skeins of plum-coloured cloud were gathering ominously in the brassy sky, while the sun hung low over the horizon like a huge disk of burnished copper and heat gripped the island in a sweaty fist.

"There's a storm coming," Thorn remarked.

Wondering if the words were prophetic, Lisa shivered and a trickle of cold perspiration ran down between her shoulderblades. At the same instant she caught sight of a tall, well-built man with fair, curly hair approaching. A moment or two later, his attention fixed on the waiting pair, he was striding across the drawbridge and mounting the steps.

His good-looking face was weary and grim, his forehead beaded with sweat. The shoes he wore were dusty, the lightweight suit creased. He had the look of someone who, pursued by devils, had travelled too far, too fast.

Thorn stepped forward but neither man spoke. After the first clash of glances they both looked at Lisa, as though waiting for her reaction.

As she stared at the man who, with her mother's wide brow and dark brown eyes, was no stranger it was as if all those years of separation had never been. They were brother and sister, the same flesh and blood, and his whole attitude confirmed what she'd been sure of from the start— he really *cared* about her.

The feeling of instant recognition and rapport filled her with warmth, banishing some of the cold dread and making her even more determined that her plan should succeed.

''Mark,'' she said gladly, and, her smile making her face radiant, she went to him. ''How marvellous to see you at last.''

As she stood on tiptoe to kiss him he made a little choked sound and hugged her close, before asking urgently, ''Are you all right?''

''I'm the happiest woman in the world! Who wouldn't be with a husband like mine?''

She turned to take Thorn's hand and draw him forward. ''Darling, come and say hello to Mark.''

It was a toss-up which of them looked the most taken aback.

Praying that they would follow her lead, Lisa waited, a bright smile pinned to her lips. When the men had nodded coolly to one another, she slipped an arm through each of theirs and, small and dainty between the two six-footers, headed for the French windows, talking gaily.

''Thorn said you'd be here as soon as you could. We were sorry you couldn't get back in time for the wedding. It was all a bit sudden, but once we realised we were in love we just couldn't wait to get married..." Blushing prettily, she gave Thorn an adoring look.

Inside, steering Mark to the nearest chair, she went on, "Come and sit down. You look tired out. But the weather's turned so hot and sticky..."

Searching for inspiration, she found it in the small bar in the corner of the room. "Thorn will get us a nice cold drink, won't you, darling?"

His green eyes ironic, he agreed, "Of course. What's it to be, darling?"

"Vodka with lots of tonic and ice."

"What about you, Mark?" Though holding no warmth, the question was polite.

Looking somewhat stunned, Mark wiped perspiration from his face and neck with a folded handkerchief and said, "I'll have the same, thanks."

While the drinks were being poured Lisa sat on the arm of her brother's chair and asked, "How did your trip go? Was it successful?"

Forced into speech, Mark began to talk about the business deals he'd made in Hong Kong.

As Thorn handed out the tall, frosted glasses, to Lisa's very great relief he asked a couple of pertinent questions, and a cool but civil conversation ensued.

When he sat down on the settee, Lisa, making a tacit statement, left her perch and went to sit by his side.

Making a statement of his own, Thorn put a possessive arm about her.

With a suddenness that almost took her by surprise, Mark broke off a description of the signing of one of the big new contracts and burst out, "I'm sorry, Lisa, I should never have gone. I bitterly regret abandoning you—"

"But you didn't abandon me," she said firmly. "You did everything in your power to make sure I was all right."

Anxious to keep the initiative, she hurried on, "And I

thought it was so good of Thorn to meet me at the airport
and let me stay with him rather than poor Mrs Simpson
having to cancel her vacation.''

Snuggling up to him, she added, ''He was absolutely
wonderful; he made certain I had everything I wanted—''

''Not quite *everything*,'' Thorn objected wickedly.

Blushing hotly, this time without any effort, she
ploughed on, ''But, best of all, he took time off to show
me Manhattan and be with me every day. And things
couldn't have worked out better.'' Taking his free hand,
she gave it a squeeze. ''It's like a dream come true. I can
still hardly believe we're really married—''

She jumped as lightning suddenly illuminated the room,
emphasising the fact that the sky had grown appreciably
darker. The flash was followed by a rumble of thunder in
the distance.

Thorn rose in one fluid movement, taking Lisa with him,
and addressed Mark crisply. ''If you're planning on getting
back to the mainland tonight you'd better not leave it too
long.'' Though politely phrased it was undoubtedly an order to go.

As she watched her brother's jaw set belligerently, the
iron bands of tension around Lisa's forehead tightened even
more. Helplessly she glanced from one man to the other.
There was anger on Mark's face, a kind of derisive watch-
fulness on Thorn's. The very air bristled with hostility.

Taking a calculated risk, she leaned against Thorn and,
gazing up at him, said, ''Oh, but he can stay here, can't he,
darling?'' She managed a coy giggle. ''I know we're on
our *honeymoon* but...''

Suddenly looking uncomfortable and uncertain, a touch
of colour appearing high on his cheekbones, Mark jumped
to his feet. ''Thanks, but I'll get on my way. I've a hotel
booked.''

She went to hug him. ''I can't thank you enough for all

your kindness and concern..." Just for an instant the real Lisa showed through.

"Look, sis," he began desperately, his grip tightening, "are you sure you know—?"

"I know you and Thorn have had your differences in the past," she broke in hastily, "but everything's going to be all right from now on." Her voice held a bright confidence that she was far from feeling.

Stepping back, she let her arms drop to her sides. "Thank you for coming and..." Momentarily she faltered, then, recovering, went on, "And take care of yourself. We'll have a proper chance to talk when Thorn and I get back to New York."

Mark's brown eyes searched her face. After a few seconds, as though not trusting himself to speak, he nodded and turned away abruptly.

A further flash lit the sky as Thorn followed the other man onto the terrace, saying coolly, "Before you go I'd better just put you in the picture with regard to CMH Electronics..."

Fighting down her agitation, Lisa watched as they stood together, Thorn speaking quietly but with obvious authority.

They were both of a height. But Mark, fair and the more conventionally handsome of the two, looked slighter, almost boyish beside Thorn's mature width of shoulder, while Thorn, dark and devilishly attractive, looked what he was—a tough, formidable man; a man to be reckoned with.

As she looked on Mark drew away and, his voice low and goaded, said, "I don't care a damn what you do to me, but you'd better be kind to *her*."

Thorn's soft, mocking laugh followed him as he descended the steps and hurried across the drawbridge.

Her stomach clenched into a knot of tension, her legs feeling like chewed string, Lisa went out onto the terrace

in time to see her brother make his way down to the bobbing boat. A moment or two later she heard the engine
splutter into life and saw the streak of blue join a small
flotilla of craft running in ahead of the storm.

It was over, and though she might have hoped to meet
her brother in less fraught circumstances it could have been
worse, she told herself shakily.

The men hadn't actually come to blows, thank God. If
they had, there was no doubt in her mind as to who would
have come off best. Though it was obvious that Mark didn't
lack guts, it was also painfully clear that he would be no
match for Thorn.

As she stood staring blindly towards the mainland a flash
of sheet-lightning was followed by a sudden spatter of rain-
drops. In the second or two it took Thorn to hurry her into
shelter the rain became so heavy that it almost drowned out
the thunder.

As he closed the French doors against the deluge, Lisa,
wiping drops from her bare arms and watching the palm-
fronds lashing about in the rising wind, began anxiously,
"Will Mark—?"

"He'll be all right," Thorn broke in trenchantly. Turning
to face her, he added with a kind of silky menace, "It's
yourself you should be worrying about."

It was undoubtedly a threat and, her blood running cold,
she stood quite still, staring at him with huge, scared eyes.

"I've a good mind to turn you over my knee for that
little performance."

She'd known from the word go that Thorn wasn't a man
to cross. But, intent on preventing a head-on clash between
the two men, and trying at the same time to ease her
brother's fears, she hadn't considered the possible consequences of her actions.

And now it was too late.

Standing in the darkened room while the storm raged

outside, she fought down a surge of panic and said with as much contempt as she could muster, ''Why not? You're a big, strong man. If you want to put yourself in the position of the pot calling the kettle black, I can't stop you. But whatever you do I've no intention of telling Mark.''

''You won't need to.''

He advanced on her, tall and dark and dangerous, and she had to use every ounce of courage she possessed to stand her ground.

Taking her chin, registering her uncontrollable flinch with a bleak smile, he tipped her face up to his. ''You might have pulled the wool over your brother's eyes to some extent with your adoring wife routine, but he's concerned enough. He knows perfectly well why I married you.''

She too knew well, but his words still had the power to turn a knife in her heart and make her want to cry with the pain.

Studying her pale, drawn face, his own expression suddenly rueful, he said with a sigh, ''You were so damn brave and gallant, defending a brother who isn't worth as much as a hair of your head.''

''He's worth *anything* and *everything* I can do for him.'' Desperately she begged, ''Can't you *see* he isn't the kind of man to ill-treat his young, pregnant wife? Somehow you just *have* to be mistaken.''

His face hardening, Thorn said curtly, ''You're forgetting that *Ginny* told me, and there's no way *she* could have been mistaken.''

Admitting to herself then that it was hopeless, that, unable to fight a ghost, she could never clear her brother's name in Thorn's book, Lisa's eyes filled with tears. Unwilling to let him see her cry, she tried hard not to blink. But, in spite of all her efforts, twin tears escaped and rolled slowly down her cheeks.

Using his thumbs to wipe them away, he remarked in a gentler tone, ''You look as if you've had enough for one day. All this emotional turmoil is obviously no good for you.'' Taking her shoulders, he pushed her gently into the nearest armchair and went through to the next room.

A short time later he reappeared to say, ''I've checked up and your brother is quite safe, if a little wet. Now try and relax while I get us something to eat.''

His unexpected solicitude made more tears spill over and run down her face in tracks of shiny wetness. Despite all his arrogance, his toughness, his occasional cruelty, he wasn't insensitive, and he could be so kind when he wanted to be, so thoughtful and considerate.

If only there had never been this trouble between the two men... If only he'd met her in different circumstances and been able to love her... But ''if only' had to be the saddest and the most futile words in the English language.

Clenching her teeth on the sobs that threatened, Lisa rubbed away the tears with her hands and struggled to regain some degree of composure.

After a while the iron bands around her forehead slowly relaxed and the tension began to seep out of her, leaving in its wake a hollow emptiness, an aching sadness.

When Thorn returned he sounded determinedly brisk and cheerful. ''It's just an oven-ready meal heated in the microwave, but come and get it.''

Feeling anything but hungry, she preceded him into the kitchen. He'd switched on the lights and she blinked in the sudden brightness.

Rain was still streaming down the windows and bouncing off the sills. She could hear it running and gurgling along the gutters and gushing in torrents from the downpipes, but the storm seemed to be moving away.

Obediently she took the chair he'd pulled out for her,

but when he began to help her to chicken and rice she half shook her head, still slightly nauseous. "I don't think—"

"You must get some food inside you," he interrupted quietly but firmly. "You've had hardly anything to eat for two days."

Pouring her a glass of white wine, he went on, "From now on I'm going to see that we enjoy our honeymoon to the full, so you'll need all your strength—" Laughing suddenly at the expression on her face, he said, "I mean for other things as well as making love…"

The gleam of white teeth, the way his lean cheeks creased, the laughing eyes made him irresistible, and her heart turned over.

"When the storm's cleared the air it will no doubt be a nice day again tomorrow, and Mrs Kirk will think we've been spending too much time in bed if we don't go home with a good tan…"

Grateful for what he was trying to do, and unable not to respond to a charm so utterly beguiling, she felt a trickle of warmth start to replace the cold, hollow feeling in the pit of her stomach.

"So some open-air pursuits are on the agenda. I intend to take you walking and sailing. And if this morning's unfortunate episode hasn't put you off, and you'd like to try snorkelling and sailboarding…?"

"Yes…yes, I would."

"Good." Lifting his glass, he saluted her courage. "I promise I'll take better care of you, and I'm sure you'll find it fun." Then coaxingly he went on, "Shall we drink to that?"

She took a sip of the chilled wine and found it deliciously light and crisp. When she set the glass down, as though she were a child he held out a forkful of chicken and urged, "Go on…"

As soon as she'd swallowed that mouthful and, under

Thorn's watchful eye, helped herself to another she found that she was ravenous. Needing no further persuasion, she cleared her plate.

Throughout the meal, while the rain stopped and the night sky cleared, he talked knowledgeably about the keys and the Florida coast. "You'll find the seabed is a fascinating place. There are all kinds of strange sea creatures, and shoals of rainbow-coloured fish dart about among exotic coral shapes and half-buried wrecks."

Enthralled, she asked, "Are there many wrecks?"

"The reefs have claimed more Spanish gold than any pirates."

As they lingered companionably over coffee and brandy Lisa found herself starting to feel tired in spite of her long sleep.

Putting a lean finger beneath her chin to prevent a yawn, his green eyes oddly gentle, Thorn murmured, "If you want to go up to bed…?"

Rising to her feet, she remarked sheepishly, "I seem to have done little else today but lie in bed and sleep."

"Oh, I don't know," he drawled and, thinking what sweet amusement it was to tease her, watched her cheeks grow pink. Dropping a light kiss on her lips, he added, "I'll be coming up myself shortly."

By the time Lisa had cleaned her teeth and prepared for bed the moon was out. Refreshed by the shower, no longer quite so sleepy, she found one of the gossamer nightdresses that Thorn had bought her and slipped it on. It felt wonderfully sensuous against her skin.

Having switched off the light, she padded barefoot to the window and, opening it, leaned with her elbows on the sill, looking out across the moon-silvered moat to the beach.

Everything was quiet; the only sounds were the hiss of the surf and the plips and plops as a million drops of water fell from trees and foliage.

The damp air was cool and fresh, the sky a clear dark blue spangled with stars, while low on the horizon the newly washed moon hung like a shining balloon. It looked as though the following day *was* going to be fine, and they could start to do all the things Thorn had suggested.

''From now on I'm going to see that we enjoy our honeymoon to the full...'' That was what he'd said.

Excitement and agitation mingling inside her, she wondered how she could be expected to enjoy a honeymoon with a man who was only using her, who didn't love her—a man she hated.

No, she didn't hate him. She had *tried* to hate him but somehow she couldn't.

Still, she hated what he'd done to her, hated the brutally casual way he had taken over her life for his own ends, hated this helpless attraction she felt for him, hated the way he *used* that attraction to defeat her will, to satisfy an appetite that *any* woman—

The thought snapped off as she remembered his contempt for his stepmother and and the hapless Carole. No, not *any* woman.

Perhaps, having been disillusioned at an early age, he felt a certain contempt for all women. Maybe he was incapable of love, of any genuine feeling, intent on just using the ones he wanted...

And he wanted her. There was no doubt about the chemistry between them.

But what would he have done if she *hadn't* appealed to him physically? Married her anyway and simply employed threats to keep her with him, instead of the double fetters of coercion and sex?

Because it had been both, she admitted to herself. She hadn't agreed to stay with him solely to protect Mark; she hadn't been *able* to leave him.

Sex, though a sensual bond, was a very strong one. She

was caught and held like a fly in a spider's web—bound with delicate, silken threads of allure...

She caught her breath in a sudden gasp. For so big a man Thorn moved lightly and gracefully and, deep in thought, she hadn't heard him coming. Sliding his arms around her, he drew her back against him. "Why are you still standing here? I'd expected you to be in bed and asleep."

"I was just looking at the night." Her voice sounded husky and impeded.

He bent his head so that his cheek rested against hers. "I thought you might be waiting for me. Were you?"

When, a shiver running through her, she stayed silent he turned her towards him and studied her face in the moonlight. "Do you *want* to sleep with me, Lisa?"

"Do I have a choice?"

With a little, twisted smile that lifted one corner of his long mouth, he said, "Yes, you have a choice."

And suddenly she had the strangest conviction that if she told him she *didn't* want to sleep with him and meant it he would respect her wishes and make no attempt to seduce her.

Taking a deep breath, she asked, "For how long?"

"For as long as you stay with me."

A chill ran through her. Perhaps she'd been wrong and he *didn't* want her. Perhaps he'd *never* really wanted her. Maybe he'd just wrapped her in those sensual bonds to give him more power over her.

Stiff lips framed the words with difficulty. "Don't you want me any more?"

"Oh, yes, I want you. *Feel* how much I want you." His hands cupped her buttocks, warm through the flimsy material, and pressed the lower half of her body to his, leaving her in no doubt that he spoke the truth.

Her throat suddenly desert-dry, she whispered, "Then *why*?"

His hands dropped, and he allowed her to put some space between them. ''Let's call it conscience because of the way I became your husband.''

''Conscience? *You*?''

His head jerked a little as though she'd slapped his face, but his voice was smooth and controlled, his words oddly formal as he went on, ''Belated, perhaps... However, I will no longer seek to be your lover unless you want me to be. The choice is yours, Lisa.''

If only he cared for her just a little, she thought despairingly. But, searching his dark face, she saw that the only emotion it held was desire. Her head drooping as though it were too heavy for her slender neck, she stared unseeingly at the small, covered buckle on his belt.

Desire. Yet how many woman would think that enough; accept what he offered and be only too glad?

Then why couldn't *she* accept what he offered? It might be her only chance of any kind of happiness. He was a generous lover, giving more than he took, and in his arms she could forget, at least for a while, the grey bleakness of a future without him.

No matter what he'd done to her, she knew now that she still loved him... The knowledge was a bitter-sweet pain— a pain that clenched around her heart like an iron fist.

But any pain he might have caused her was easily outweighed by the ecstasy he'd given her. And in her soul she knew that he was the only man for her, the only man she had ever loved, and ever *would* love.

Lifting her head, she looked him in the face and said clearly, ''Yes, I want you to be my lover.''

For an instant he stood quite still, as though transfixed, then the tension snapped. With an incoherent murmur he drew her close and, his lips muffled against her scented hair, held her so tightly that she felt as if her ribs might crack beneath the weight and pressure of his arms.

Perhaps she made some small protest because his grip relaxed and, sounding oddly breathless, he said, "Sorry, darling, was I hurting you?"

"Yes…no…it doesn't matter. I *want* you to hold me."

He held her a moment or two longer, his cheek against hers, then, drawing away, he looked at her. What he saw in her face was a potent aphrodisiac—had he needed one; it made him feel like Suleiman.

Reaching out, he removed the pins from her hair, and smiled as the riot of silky curls came tumbling around her shoulders.

A man who knew how to wait for his pleasures, slowly, savouring the moment, he slid the thin straps of the night-dress from her shoulders and let it fall in a silken drift around her feet. Moonlight washed her thighs, her shoulders, the pale curves of her breasts.

She was lovely, he thought; delicate as a piece of fine porcelain yet warm and courageous and strong, with a spirit of pure steel.

Apparently content for the moment to look, he was making no effort to touch her, but, almost deafened by the beating of her own heart, she was *aware* of him with every single nerve in her body.

Then where the moonlight had been his hands followed, their light touch bringing a heart-stopping excitement. For a moment she watched them, well-shaped and strong, dark against her pale flesh, before lifting her face to his.

Their mouths met and clung, and a current of desire flowed between them, so strong that it swept them both away. He lifted her and laid her on the moonlit carpet before stripping off his own clothes with fingers grown suddenly urgent.

As she watched him standing there, as naked and beautiful as some Greek statue, Lisa's breath caught in her throat and she lifted eager arms to pull him down to her.

He kissed her eyelids, her hair, her parted lips, her breasts, while, with a perfect knowledge of her needs, he stroked and caressed her until she was mindless with wanting.

When he finally covered her body with his own he made no attempt to shield her from his weight, knowing instinctively that she hungered for it.

Their loving was swift and fierce and incandescent, the climax of joy almost insupportable.

While their heartbeats and breathing returned to normal they lay quietly, his dark head heavy on her breast. Then, the cool air from the window chilling their heated bodies, he roused himself and, gathering her into his arms, carried her over to the bed. Holding her close, he settled her head on his shoulder and said softly, ''Sleep now, my love.''

''My love''…

But she wasn't his love—just a woman who pleased him. Even though he hated her brother. And when he'd had enough of revenge and she ceased to please him, because there was no deeper feeling, no bond of affection, he would eventually let her go.

She lay listening to his quiet, even breathing, and while her body still sang from his lovemaking her heart wept tears of blood.

CHAPTER TEN

HAVING extended their stay on Jacob's Island by several days, Thorn and Lisa returned, fit and tanned, to New York in a blistering heat that made even the slightest fume-laden breeze welcome.

Mrs Kirk, wearing yellow tracksuit bottoms and a scarlet and green T-shirt, welcomed them back with her usual dour enthusiasm.

"There's a meal waiting for you, and I've made space for Mrs Landers' things in the master bedroom. You will be sharing, I take it? It's not to be one of these modern marriages where the couple have separate rooms?"

"Indeed it's not," Thorn assured her, with a teasing glance at Lisa that made her blush and wish they were still alone.

Nodding her stern approval, the housekeeper was departing when she paused to say, "Oh, and while you were away Miss Guggenheim—" an eloquent sniff made it plain what she thought of that young woman "—phoned to remind you about a party next Saturday night. I made it clear that you were on honeymoon, but she still insisted that you'd promised to go.

"And Mr Hayward has rung several times to ask if you were back..."

At the mention of Mark Thorn's strong-boned face grew set and cold. When he'd carried their cases through to the bedroom he said abruptly, "As soon as I've showered and changed I'm going into the office. Can you find something to do while I'm gone?''

Chilled by his tone, Lisa answered, ''Of course. But aren't you going to eat first?''

''I'll have some sandwiches sent in if I want anything.''

A bare ten minutes later, with a curt, ''I don't know what time I'll be back, so don't wait up for me,'' he was gone, and she was left alone, her bubble of happiness burst like a pricked balloon.

While they had been away, pushing all worries about the future to the back of her mind, she'd treasured each day as though it was a priceless gift, living and laughing and loving, giving everything she had to give, holding nothing back.

As though he'd also temporarily banished his demons, Thorn had looked younger and handsomer than ever, a glow about him that could have been mistaken for happiness.

Their days had been spent in walking and water sports, lounging on the beach and reading, their nights in making long, leisurely, satisfying love.

Thorn had usually fixed breakfast, which, sometimes conversing, sometimes kissing, they'd eaten in bed, as often as not lingering to make love again afterwards.

Having known many overtly sexy women who had turned out to be cold and calculating, he had been elated by her warmth and passion—the tiger lurking beneath that innocent, wholesome, girl-next-door appearance—and he had told her so.

Though both comfortable with silence, they'd talked a great deal, discussing anything and everything, agreeing most of the time, enjoying the verbal cut and thrust when they disagreed. The only things they had never discussed were Mark and the shadow that lay over their relationship.

Managing with impromptu lunches and picnics, they had

spent a lot of their time exploring, and, though she was scrupulous in her personal habits, a shiny nose, salt-tangled hair and mud-caked feet from paddling round the mangroves trying to spot tiny crabs and mud-hoppers hadn't bothered Lisa in the slightest.

Used to bored, jejune women who seemed unable to function without a daily visit to the beauty parlour and a constant check on their looks, Thorn had been delighted by Lisa's intellect, her enthusiastic love of life and her complete lack of vanity, and once again he'd told her so, raising hopes that one day he might come to care.

They had taken it in turns to prepare the evening meal— a meal which had quite often been delayed when, after a day in the sun, Thorn had had more important things on his mind than food.

During the second week he'd asked if she would like to visit the keys, but when, their time alone being precious to her, she'd answered, "Only if you do," he had seemed glad to drop the subject.

She hadn't felt the need for company or night-life, and, insular as their existence had been, it was as close to paradise as Lisa had ever expected to get.

Now suddenly she was back to earth, and with their return to New York and real life Thorn was all at once a different man from her carefree island lover, and her fragile hopes were dashed.

Over the next few days she scarcely saw him as he worked from early morning until late at night—a punishing routine that, even with his magnificent constitution, made him look weary.

Though they slept in the same bed he made no effort to touch her, and treated her with a cool politeness that almost broke her heart. Perhaps if she'd approached him things might have been different, but, much as she wanted to be in his arms, her pride wouldn't allow her to beg.

At the first opportunity she'd rung Mark's flat and got an answering machine that told her he'd had to go to California on business. She had left a message asking him to call as soon as he got back.

It was Friday evening before the phone rang.

"Lisa?"

"Mark!" she exclaimed gladly. "When did you get home?"

"About ten minutes ago. Look, can I see you?"

"Of course. When?"

"I suppose you can't get away now?"

"Yes…yes, I can." Mrs Kirk was out and Lisa had been about to eat a solitary meal in the kitchen. Hurriedly she added, "Thorn's working late. He had a lot to catch up on."

"Dinner, then? Can you grab a cab and meet me at Fingles in about half an hour?"

"Where's that?"

"Madison and Sixty-seventh Street."

"I'll be there."

Losing not a moment, Lisa called a cab. By the time she'd changed into an elegant black cocktail dress and got down to the main entrance it was waiting.

Fingles was a select, ground-floor restaurant with beautifully draped windows and a liveried doorman. As the cab drew up outside she saw that Mark was already there, waiting for her beneath the green and gold canopy.

Hurrying forward, he helped her out and paid the cabby before escorting her through the smoked-glass doors which the commissionaire was holding open for them.

Air-conditioning made the pale green and gold room refreshingly cool, while several large flower arrangements added bright splashes of colour. The place appeared to be fairly full, most of the tables occupied by a very well-dressed clientele.

Mark murmured a few words to the head waiter and a twenty-dollar bill discreetly changed hands. A moment later they were being shown to a secluded booth in an alcove.

Thorn could scarcely have managed it more smoothly, Lisa thought as they were seated and handed menus.

As soon as they were alone Mark's troubled brown eyes searched her face. "Are you all right?"

"I'm fine," she told him.

"You don't look very happy," he observed shrewdly. Then, with a sigh, he said, "I wish we'd had time to really get to know one another."

"So do I. But we'll have time in the future."

"I doubt it. Thorn hates my guts. He won't like us meeting, and he's not a man to cross." Mark's hand was clenched on the table, the knuckles showing white. "If he finds out about tonight he'll probably be furious, and he might—"

She covered his hand with her own, stopping the anxious words. "You don't need to worry."

"I wish I could be certain of that."

"You can."

"But he only married you to—" Mark broke off abruptly.

Calmly she said, "I *know* why he married me. But no matter what he might want *you* to believe he won't hurt me." Not physically at least...she thought.

Sounding shaken, Mark asked, "If you know why he married you, why don't you leave him?"

"Because I love him." It was the truth, if not the *whole* of it.

"He's a dangerous man to love," Mark said sombrely. "A hard and ruthless man... Do you know about Ginny—?" He stopped speaking abruptly as a waiter appeared at his elbow.

As soon as they had given their order and were alone again Lisa said quietly, "Yes, I know about Ginny."

"She was a beautiful girl, cheerful and high-spirited. We hadn't been married very long when for some reason Thorn got it into his head that I was knocking her about—"

"Were you?"

"Good Lord, no! I loved her. Though I soon came to realise our marriage had been a mistake, I would *never* have lifted a finger to her." There was an unmistakable ring of truth in his voice. "But I couldn't make Thorn believe that. Because she had a bruise on her arm he damn near broke my jaw.

"I don't know *why*, or what the hell was going on, but somehow things went from bad to worse. I couldn't do anything to please her, and after she lost the baby he persuaded her to leave me. I wondered if he—" Mark stopped speaking abruptly.

After a moment Lisa said quietly, "It's not what you think. He believes you pushed her down the stairs while you were quarrelling."

"Dear God!" Mark sounded horrified. "I admit we *were* quarrelling that night, but she slipped. I was nowhere near her when she fell; Carole must surely know that."

"*Carole*?"

"A friend of Ginny's. They were very thick, even after we got married."

Savagely he added, "I always thought she was a bad influence. I wish to God that Thorn *had* fancied the girl. She was absolutely mad about him, and *he* might have been able to keep her out of trouble."

So that was how Carole fitted in, Lisa thought.

"Which was more than Sol Guggenheim could do. Though he lavished endless money on her, gave her everything she wanted, he let her run wild."

Her heart beating faster, Lisa got back to the really important bit. "And you mean Ginny would have told Carole what happened that night?"

"I mean Carole was *there*. In fact she was the reason why the quarrel started. She wanted Ginny to go with her to one of those wild parties they were so fond of. But Ginny looked pale and ill that night and I didn't want her to go." At that moment their food arrived. While it was being served, hiding the nervous excitement that filled her, Lisa tried to sort out her thoughts. She was convinced that Mark had spoken the truth. But in that case why had Ginny made her brother think the worst, set the two men at each other's throat?

When the waiter finally moved away Lisa made a determined effort to change the subject, trying to banish the bleakness from Mark's fair face.

"You said in one of your letters that as a toddler I used to climb on your knee, and I think I can remember. Didn't you once...?"

Throughout the rest of the meal and while they lingered over coffee they talked about their childhood, and caught up on each other's life.

It was Mark who finally realised how late it was getting. Agitatedly he hurried her outside and waved down a cab. "Shall I go with you? What if he—?"

"I doubt if he'll be home," she said soothingly. "He's been at the office till all hours since we got back. Thank you for the meal. I'll be in touch." She gave him a swift hug and dived into the cab.

The penthouse was dusky and silent when she let herself in. She was halfway across the shadowy living-room when a tall figure uncoiled itself from a chair, bringing a gasp to her throat. A second later the lights flashed on.

"Where the hell have you been?" Thorn demanded. He was tieless and in his shirtsleeves, his dark face a mask of anger.

"Out." She faced him defiantly.

Green eyes glittering, he snarled, "I don't need to ask who with."

"Mark took me for a meal."

Briefly she wondered whether to tell Thorn what her brother had said, then decided against it. It was still only his word against Ginny's. But if she could get Carole to corroborate Mark's story...

Seeing Thorn's jaw clench, she said recklessly, "You didn't order me not to see him."

"And if I had?"

"You're not home enough to make a good gaoler," she taunted. "For the past four nights I've eaten alone—" the resentment spilt over "—and I might as well have slept alone for all the notice you've taken of me."

"A poor, neglected little wife," Thorn mocked. "But I don't intend to neglect you any longer." His meaning was unmistakable.

With a swift, unexpected movement he swept her up in his arms and carried her through to their bedroom where it was dim but not dark.

"Leave me alone." She began to struggle furiously. "I'm going to sleep in my old room."

"Oh, no, my darling." He was coldly, quietly furious. "I plan to make love to you until you're begging for mercy and I'm sated."

"I'd sooner you beat me," she cried.

"I doubt it."

Tossing her contemptuously onto the big divan, he switched on the bedside lamp, bathing her in a pool of light, and began to unbutton his shirt.

Scrambling off the other side, she made a run for the door. Before she had covered a quarter of the distance she was caught and dragged back.

Fighting and kicking, hearing the seams of her dress tear, she was mercilessly stripped.

"I hate you," she sobbed. "I *hate* you."

"What's new?" Restraining her with one arm, he discarded the rest of his clothes.

A moment later she was spread-eagled on the bed and he was pinning her down, controlling her movements.

"I'll *scream*," she choked.

"You'll have to scream very loudly. Mrs Kirk's out, helping to run a midnight movie screening to raise funds for the homeless. Now, my sweet little termagant…"

She shivered once, convulsively, when he first touched her, then, a fatalistic calm enveloping her, she lay still and silent, her head turned away, passive as a rag doll, while his hands travelled over her.

It wasn't his style to take her roughly, just to satisfy himself and leave her unmoved. It wouldn't suit his ego, she thought bitterly. And obviously he wanted to punish her, to have her writhing and whimpering beneath him, made a helpless, quivering mass by the exquisite, sensual torture he could inflict.

But where sex was concerned the body didn't function alone; the mind had to be involved to sharpen those sensations the way a steel whetted a knife. So if her only defence was detachment she would use it, and he could have the shell that was her body.

His hands stilled and, as if clairvoyant, he took her chin in one hand and turned her face to his. Her clear hazel eyes held a curious blind blankness, as though she looked through him.

Almost regretfully he said, "That won't work, my darling wife. I shall make sure your mind stays to help you enjoy what I'm going to do to you now."

He nipped her bottom lip between his strong white teeth

and, smiling, watched the pupils of her eyes dilate and darken involuntarily.

When Lisa awoke and stretched the bed was empty and daylight filled the room. Waves of heat that turned into shivers ran through her as, racked by humiliation, she remembered the previous night.

Her struggles had proved ineffectual; her attempts to distance herself from what was happening to her had provoked nothing but a mocking laugh.

Making himself master of her body, he had used her with taunting insolence and, smiling as he watched her writhe and become a helpless slave to passion, trodden her pride into the dust.

She would never forgive him, she vowed. Never!

Her throat dry, needing a cup of coffee, she pulled on a light dressing-gown and padded through to the kitchen.

Mrs Kirk, her grey hair rumpled, her steel-rimmed glasses slightly awry, was preparing lunch. Sourly she remarked, ''It seems we both overslept.''

''Thorn—'' Lisa said his name with difficulty ''—mentioned you were at a midnight screening, so you've got a good excuse.''

''Aye, but I've a lot to do today—'' The phone shrilled through Mrs Kirk's words and, muttering darkly, she went to answer it.

Lisa had poured herself a coffee and was drinking it gratefully when the housekeeper returned, looking wrathful. ''It was that Miss Guggenheim again, wanting to remind Mr Landers about tonight's party. I told her he was at his office. She knows better than to bother him there.''

Carefully Lisa remarked, ''I understand she was a friend of Ginny's?''

The housekeeper gave her a guarded look. ''So she was.''

Lisa threw caution to the winds. "Mrs Kirk, what was Ginny like? *Really* like, I mean." Seeing the reluctance on the housekeeper's face, she went on desperately, "This isn't just idle curiosity. I *need* to know, and you are the one person who could give me an unbiased opinion."

There was a lengthy silence, and Lisa had just decided that her appeal had failed, when Mrs Kirk said flatly, "As a child she was as pretty as a picture, bright and fetching and amenable when it suited her, but a terrible liar, sly and underhand and set on having her own way.

"I did my best, and no one should speak ill of the dead, but she grew up to be wild and no better than she should be. Many's the scrape she's got into and had to hide from her brother.

"He was too busy building up the business to see what was going on, and she could wind him round her little finger. He'd never believe any wrong of her. But I didn't like the way she used to flaunt—"

Mrs Kirk broke off abruptly. After a moment she went on, "It was a great relief when she got married, though I felt sorry for Mr Hayward... But there! I've probably said too much and it's not my place to—"

An impulsive hug stopped the housekeeper's apology. "Thank you for being so frank. I won't repeat a word."

Mrs Kirk shrugged her bony shoulders. "Maybe it's time it was said. And I've just told the truth."

Lisa clenched her teeth. Somehow at tonight's party she must persuade Carole to do the same...

While she was helping Mrs Kirk clear away the lunch things, her mind still on the party, Lisa recalled that it was to be at the prestigious Waldorf-Astoria.

Though she felt upset and angry over the way Thorn had treated her, a kind of perverse pride made her hate the idea of letting him down in front of his friends.

"I should have had something done with my face and hair." She spoke her thoughts aloud.

"There's a hairdressing and beauty salon just by the leisure area," Mrs Kirk suggested.

Lisa sighed. "It's probably too late now to make an appointment, and in any case I...I forgot to ask Thorn for any money."

With a better grasp of the weight that the Landers name carried, Mrs Kirk exclaimed, "Och, away with you! I'll give them a ring and they'll send Mr Landers the bill."

It was five-thirty before Lisa emerged from the beautician's looking and feeling like a different woman.

The curly, sun-streaked hair had been cut into a short style that made her neck appear longer and showed to advantage her beautiful bone structure. Her skin glowed and her nails had a pearly sheen, while a professional make-up emphasised her mouth and eyes, turning her into a raving beauty.

Though her own assessment was a great deal more modest, she felt, looking in the mirror, confident that she could go anywhere without fear of disgracing him.

When six o'clock came and there was still no sign of Thorn Lisa began to feel anxious. Had he decided not to go to the party after all?

Picking up the phone, she dialled his office number and waited. It rang a couple of times before he answered brusquely, "Landers speaking."

"I wondered what time you would be home."

Somehow she got the impression that he was startled to hear her voice, but after a moment he asked with cool derision, "Hoping to sneak out again to meet that brother of yours?"

Knowing it would defeat the object to quarrel, Lisa held onto her temper. "Miss Guggenheim rang earlier to remind you about the party tonight... You are going, aren't you?"

"I'm in no mood for a party," he said irritably.

"*Please*, Thorn, won't you take me? I've had my hair done specially, and I'd really like to go." She held her breath.

"Very well, as you beg so prettily." Then, almost to himself, he said "And if Carole is made to face the fact that I have a wife it may cure her obsession."

For the first time Lisa thought of it from the other girl's point of view. Guiltily she said, "I don't want it to spoil her party. She can't help loving you and I—"

"Surely you're not still naïve enough to talk about *love*? There's infatuation and good, honest desire, but there's no such thing as love—at least not in the way you mean." Curtly he added, "I'll be home in about an hour."

Her relief mingling with anxiety, Lisa chose the most stunning gown Thorn had bought for her—gold lamé with shoe-string straps. It was deceptively simple, cinching her slender waist and flowing smoothly over her rounded hips; if it showed rather more of her cleavage than she would have liked, by current standards it was modest.

High-heeled strappy sandals, a wrap and a matching bag completed her ensemble. She wore no jewellery except Thorn's pendant and her engagement ring. Ready, she waited in an agony of suspense.

When he hadn't arrived home by seven-thirty she was in despair, certain that he'd changed his mind. But then, to her great relief she heard the outer door open and close.

He was walking past her with scarcely a glance when he stopped abruptly and demanded, "What the *hell* have you done to yourself?"

His attack was so savage, so unexpected that her eyes filled with tears. "I...I didn't want to let you down..."

"For God's sake don't cry." Wearily he added, "It's just that I prefer your hair long, and I'm sick to death of the plastic clones beauticians turn out."

With a short, sharp sigh he turned on his heel and headed for the bedroom, saying over his shoulder, ''I'll be with you in about fifteen minutes.''

By the time he returned, looking strikingly handsome in his evening clothes, Lisa had herself well under control. Though churning inside with dismay and disappointment, and anxiety over what she hoped to do, she was once more outwardly cool and composed.

When they reached the Waldorf the party seemed to be in full swing, with a constant swirl of talk and laughter, a band playing for those who wished to dance, and champagne flowing like Niagara.

It was a glittering affair with the cream of New York society present—the women dazzling in jewels and haute couture gowns, the men wearing evening dress and an unmistakable air of wealth and power.

As they made their way towards their hostess a number of the most powerful men on Wall Street greeted Thorn with respect. Smiling, playing the part of a proud husband, he introduced Lisa and accepted their congratulations and accusations of being a sly dog with urbanity.

Carole, accompanied by a short, stout man with thick, rubbery lips, came to meet them. Wearing a daring scarlet dress that suited her dark beauty, she smiled brilliantly, ''Thorn, darling, I'm so delighted to see you.''

She seemed about to kiss him when, with smooth politeness, he took her hand and raised it to his lips before releasing it. ''You've met Lisa, haven't you?''

''Yes, of course.'' With a noticeable lack of enthusiasm, Carole added, ''Nice of you to come.''

''Landers...'' The short, stout man held out his hand.

When the men had shaken hands, Thorn said smoothly, turning to Lisa, ''Darling, I'd like you to meet Sol Guggenheim, Carole's father... Sol, this is my wife, Lisa.''

The pudgy hand clasped hers and the dark eyes, embedded in their folds of flesh, narrowed. To Thorn he said, "I had no idea you were married...and to such a beautiful girl."

"It was a whirlwind romance. We kept everything quiet because of the Press."

"Hi there!" A large, fair-haired young man suddenly appeared on the scene and held out a sizeable paw.

Recognising him as the man Carole had been with when they'd met in Sky Windows, Lisa smiled and said, "Hello, Paul."

When he'd shaken hands with her and Thorn he said to Carole, "Coming to dance, honey?" Seeming not to notice her sullen reluctance, he put a beefy arm around her and drew her away.

Staring after them, Sol Guggenheim asked, "What do you think of him?"

"A pleasant and singularly determined young man," Thorn answered.

Sol nodded slowly. "He may well become my son-in-law. I believe he loves Carole, and he seems to know how to handle her... Ah, there's Manny...I'll leave you two to start enjoying the party."

As their host moved away Thorn bent his dark head to ask, "Would you like to dance, darling?" and in her turn Lisa found herself led onto the polished floor.

Normally she loved dancing with him, but tonight, with so much wrong between them and her mind on other things, she found herself unable to relax, and was relieved when he suggested circulating.

Two hours and several glasses of champagne later Lisa seemed no nearer to achieving what she'd set out to do. Thorn had never left her side, and whether it was due to pique or Paul's influence she wasn't sure, but Carole had given them a wide berth.

People had started to drift towards the buffet, and after

finding them a seat in a quiet alcove Thorn asked, "Hungry?"

"Starving," Lisa lied.

"Then I'll go and see what I can find."

As soon as he'd walked away Lisa began to search the crowd for that bright splash of scarlet. If only she could spot Carole and get her alone for a minute...

Then, as if the wish had conjured her up, the dark girl appeared by Lisa's side. A touch unsteady on her feet, the glass in her hand tilting dangerously, Carole sat down on the blue velvet settee and demanded, "Congratulate me, why don't you? Paul and I have just got engaged."

"I hope you'll be very happy," Lisa said sincerely. "Paul seems really nice."

"Oh, he is," Carole said bitterly. "But *you've* got the only man I've ever really wanted. I tried...God, how I tried...to get him to love me, and I wasn't the *only* one, but when it comes to women he's a cruel, arrogant swine."

Don't I know it? Lisa thought.

"How did you get him to love you?" Carole demanded, her speech slightly slurred. "I'd like to know the secret—"

"But he *doesn't* love me." Instinctively Lisa chose the truth. "He only married me to get back at Mark."

Her eyes looking as if she was having trouble focusing, Carole frowned. "Mark?"

"I'm Mark Hayward's sister."

"I never knew he had a sister. So what?"

"Thorn believes Mark ill-treated Ginny and—"

"That's a laugh!" Carole swallowed the rest of her champagne and let the empty glass slip from her hand and roll onto the thick carpet. "Shows how blind and stupid even the most intelligent men can be. Ginny had Mark on a string; he was besotted with her and she didn't care two hoots about him. She'd never wanted him—"

"But she was carrying his baby."

"It wasn't Mark's baby, it was Rick Merryl's. He was even younger than Ginny but an absolute tearaway, always in trouble with the police. He's the one who got her started on drugs—"

Like someone in a daze, Lisa repeated, "It wasn't Mark's baby?"

"Of course it wasn't. She was pregnant before she ever slept with him. That was one of the reasons why she married him—she was scared of Thorn finding out who the baby's real father was. He'd have been *furious* and—"

Afraid of Thorn coming back before she'd got at the truth, Lisa broke in hurriedly, "You were there the night she fell downstairs and lost the baby?"

"I'd called to take her to a party; I thought she needed cheering up. He didn't want her to go and they quarrelled about it."

"But Mark says he was nowhere near her when she accidentally slipped."

"She didn't slip and it was no accident…"

All Lisa's hopes came crashing around her so that she scarcely heard Carole's next few words. When the sense of them began to penetrate she whispered urgently, "Say that again."

"I said she did it on purpose."

"*She* did it on purpose? But *why*? Why on earth would she do such a thing?"

"To try and hide the fact that earlier in the day she'd sneaked off to a back street abortionist…"

Seeing Lisa's horrified face, Carole muttered, "I told her she was being a fool. She'd wanted to get rid of it from the start, but not only was she scared, she was afraid that if she went to a reputable clinic Thorn would find out.

"And she couldn't have that. The thing that mattered most in the world was that he thought well of her, that he loved her. And I don't mean like a brother…

"The other reason why she'd married Mark was to make Thorn jealous, and when that didn't seem to work she got even more restless and unhappy. She wanted to be with Thorn but she didn't want to go back carrying another man's baby.

"Everything she did was because of Thorn. She wanted him to see her as a desirable woman, to *want* her. They weren't blood relations, you know, and she'd been mad about him for years. But he'd always treated her like a child and it drove her mad—"

"Oh, God, I think I'm going to be sick…" Lisa stumbled to her feet.

A strong arm went round her and steered her towards the cloakroom. Summoning one of the female attendants, Thorn said urgently, "Will you take care of my wife? She's feeling unwell."

Only too thankful that she hadn't eaten, Lisa slowly sipped a glass of water, and when the nausea began to subside she smiled wanly at the elderly woman who was hovering solicitously by her chair and said, "I'm fine now, thank you. I'd better go back."

Thorn was standing just outside the door, his eyes like dark holes cut in a mask. He had collected her bag and wrap, and without a word he hurried her straight out to a waiting taxi.

The journey to the penthouse was completed in silence, and not until she was sitting in a chair in the living-room did he open his mouth to ask, "Would you like a brandy?"

She shook her head.

He poured himself a glass and swallowed it straight down. Then he said curtly, "You look like a ghost. I suggest you go to bed."

Again she shook her head. "We need to talk." Her voice sounded thin and reedy.

"We'll talk later. There's something I have to do first.

Go and get some rest, Lisa.'' He walked away, and she heard the outer door click to behind him.

Curiously numb, neither thinking nor feeling, she stayed where she was, sitting in the chair like a zombie while the minutes ticked past and lengthened into hours.

She must have dozed, because she opened heavy eyes to find Thorn standing looking down at her, grey-faced and weary, still in evening dress.

Chilled and stiff, she saw that the first pale streaks of dawn were fingering the sky. ''I'll make some coffee,'' she said huskily.

But when she attempted to rise he pushed her gently back. ''I'll do it.''

He returned quite quickly and, having handed her a steaming mug, sat down opposite. The coffee was hot and strong and reviving, and they drank without speaking.

It was Lisa who broke the silence. ''How much did you overhear?''

''Most of it. I saw Carole come and sit beside you. It was obvious that she was more than a little drunk and I thought she might try out her claws, so I came back.''

''Did you believe what she said?''

''I didn't want to. When I left you I went over to the hospital. Because it was the middle of the night it wasn't easy, but finally I managed to get someone to check the medical records. Ginny—'' his voice cracked on the name ''—didn't lose the baby because of her fall. She was no longer pregnant when she was admitted.

''I feel so damn guilty. I ought to have seen that she was sick. Ought to have been able to help her.''

So he was still only thinking of Ginny.

Coldly Lisa asked, ''What about Mark? Don't you feel guilty about misjudging *him*? About all the rotten things you've said and done?''

His face bleak, Thorn said, ''When I left the hospital I

went over to see him. He wasn't thrilled at being knocked up at three o'clock in the morning, but after he'd calmed down enough to listen to what I had to say we had a frank talk.

"I told him I'll willingly make what reparation I can, and as far as *his* affairs go he's very forgiving. It's *you* he's worried about. And so am I."

"How nice of you."

"If you want to leave me—"

She laughed harshly. "*If* I want to leave you!"

A muscle jerked in his jaw. "I'll give you a house, a car, a cash settlement, a monthly income, anything you—"

"I don't want a house or a car or your money," she broke in icily. "All I want is to go to Mark." She struggled to her feet.

Catching her arm, Thorn said urgently, "Wait until you're not so tired, until you've had time to think—"

"I don't need to think." She pulled herself free and headed for the door. She was halfway through it when his low, impassioned voice halted her.

"Lisa, don't go." The words were simple, but then he wasn't a man to beg.

Lifting her chin, she closed the door behind her and took the lift down. Her heels clicked and echoed in the emptiness as she crossed the lobby and let herself out.

Standing on the sidewalk in her beautiful gold lamé gown, she looked up and down Fifth Avenue. In a short time it would wake and erupt into bustling life, but now, in the early dawn, it was eerily quiet and deserted.

Then, a block or so away, she spotted a yellow cab dropping off some late revellers. She could be with Mark in a few minutes.

But did she really want to be? She'd thought of herself and Mark as the only innocent parties, but Thorn was innocent too. All he'd done was believe the lies that a sick girl had fed him.

When she let herself back in the security guard, who had appeared in the lobby, gave her a startled look, then, recognising her, a polite salute. "Good morning, Mrs Landers."

"Good morning." Her answering smile was serene and sunny.

She let herself quietly into the penthouse and found Thorn sitting where she'd left him, his elbows on his knees, his dark head sunk in his hands.

Perhaps she made some slight sound, because he looked up, and she read such misery, such bleak desolation on his tired face that she winced.

The despair was instantly masked. Rising to his feet, he asked coolly, "Forgotten something?"

"Yes."

He raised a questioning brow.

"I'd forgotten how much I love you," she said simply. "I don't mean *want*, I mean *love*—the kind you don't believe in."

A second later he'd closed the gap between them and she was crushed against him. His mouth muffled against her hair, he groaned.

"When I realised what a fool I'd been, how I'd let Ginny pull the wool over my eyes and nearly wreck all our lives, my only hope was that you *did* feel more for me than mere passion. That way there was a chance you might forgive me.

"But it wasn't until I knew I'd lost you that I finally admitted to myself that what I felt went a great deal deeper than just *wanting* you. If love means caring and tenderness and affection, feeling a strong and lasting commitment, then I love you."

She drew away a little and, her eyes full of happy tears,

teased, "I'm not sure I can take it in just yet. Let's go to bed and you can keep telling me until I do."

"Only *tell*? Can't I *show* you how much I love you?"

Taking his hand, she led him towards the bedroom. "Yes, please."

The world's bestselling romance series.

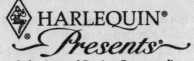

Seduction and Passion Guaranteed!

They're the men who have everything— except a bride...

Wealth, power, charm—what else could a
heart-stoppingly handsome tycoon need? In the
GREEK TYCOONS miniseries you have already
been introduced to some gorgeous Greek
multimillionaires who are in need of wives.

Bestselling author *Jacqueline Baird* presents
THE GREEK TYCOON'S REVENGE
Harlequin Presents, #2266
Available in August

Marcus had found Eloise and he wants revenge—by
making Eloise his mistress for one year!

This tycoon has met his match, and he's decided he *has* to
have her...*whatever* that takes!

**Pick up a Harlequin Presents® novel and you will
enter a world of spine-tingling passion and
provocative, tantalizing romance!**

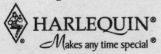

The world's bestselling romance series.

HARLEQUIN®
Presents

Seduction and Passion Guaranteed!

A new trilogy by **Carole Mortimer**

BACHELOR COUSINS

Three cousins of Scottish descent...they're male, millionaires and marriageable!

Meet Logan, Fergus and Brice, three tall, dark, handsome men about town. They've made their millions in London, but their hearts belong to the heather-clad hills of their grandfather McDonald's Scottish estate.

Logan, Fergus and Brice are about to give up their keenly fought-for bachelor status for three wonderful women— laugh, cry and read all about their trials and tribulations in their pursuit of love.

To Marry McKenzie
On-sale July, #2261

Look out for:
To Marry McCloud
On-sale August, #2267

To Marry McAllister
On-sale September, #2273

Pick up a Harlequin Presents novel and you will enter a world of spine-tingling passion and provocative, tantalizing romance!

HARLEQUIN®
Makes any time special ®

Available wherever Harlequin books are sold.

HPBACH2

The world's bestselling romance series.

HARLEQUIN®
Presents

Seduction and Passion Guaranteed!

SOCIETY WEDDINGS

**They're gorgeous, they're glamorous...
and they're getting married!**

Be our VIP guest at two of the most-talked-about
weddings of the decade—lavish ceremonies where the
cream of society gather to celebrate these marriages
in dazzling international settings.

Welcome to the sensuous, scandalous world
of the rich, royal and renowned!

SOCIETY WEDDINGS
Two original short stories in one volume:

Promised to the Sheikh
by *Sharon Kendrick*

The Duke's Secret Wife
by *Kate Walker*
on sale August, #2268

**Pick up a Harlequin Presents® novel and you will
enter a world of spine-tingling passion and
provocative, tantalizing romance!**

HARLEQUIN®
Makes any time special ®

*Available wherever
Harlequin books
are sold.*

Coming Next Month...

A special promotion from

HARLEQUIN®
Presents

Seduction and Passion Guaranteed!

Details to follow in September 2002 Harlequin Presents books.

Don't miss it!